'You're not wanted for three weeks, Dr Russell.'

He shook his head. 'You can take yourself off to your texts—or sleep by the swimming-pool for all I care. But you're not working.'

'But——'

'Beattie has explained things to me,' Luke went on blandly. 'She tells me you're set on passing this exam and it's my responsibility to see that you do.'

'I'm not your responsibility. . .'

'No. But your practice is.'

Dear Reader

In Australia, Marion Lennox has Nikki and Luke find a STORM HAVEN; Laura MacDonald's Toni finds herself IN AT THE DEEP END with her new boss in Africa; at the health centre, Margaret O'Neill's Dr Ben Masters becomes NO LONGER A STRANGER to Clare Lucas; and we meet Michael Knight again— first seen in PRIDE'S FALL—in Flora Sinclair's KNIGHT'S MOVE as he meets his match in Jessica Balfour. Happy New Year!

The Editor

Marion Lennox has had a variety of careers—medical receptionist, computer programmer and teacher. Married, with two young children, she now lives in rural Victoria, Australia. Her wish for an occupation which would allow her to remain at home with her children, her dog and the budgie led her to attempt writing a novel, and she has now published several.

Recent titles by the same author:

ONE CARING HEART
LEGACY OF SHADOWS
A LOVING LEGACY

STORM
HAVEN

BY
MARION LENNOX

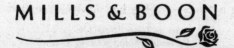

MILLS & BOON LIMITED
ETON HOUSE, 18-24 PARADISE ROAD
RICHMOND, SURREY TW9 1SR

*First published in Great Britain 1994
by Mills & Boon Limited*

© Marion Lennox 1994

*Australian copyright 1994   Philippine copyright 1995
This edition 1995*

ISBN 0 263 78915 2

*Set in Times 10 on 10½ pt. by
Rowland Phototypesetting Limited
Bury St Edmunds, Suffolk*

03-9501-49343

Made and printed in Great Britain

CHAPTER ONE

'NIKKI RUSSELL, you're killing yourself!'

Nikki looked up from her books. The causes of renal failure were swimming around her tired mind, and it took a moment before she could focus on her elderly housekeeper. Beattie Gilchrist stalked forward and planted a mug of hot chocolate on top of Nikki's open text. 'I know you asked for coffee,' she said darkly, 'but I've no intention of helping you stay awake. It's bed you need, Dr Russell, and that's a fact.'

Nikki smiled wearily and pushed her heavy glasses from her nose. 'Thanks, Beattie. I'm coming to bed in a moment.'

'I know. I know.' Mrs Gilchrist folded her arms and glared at her employer. 'In a few hours more like. You delivered the Raymond baby last night, you were up at six to Amy, you had a full day at the surgery today and it's near to midnight now. Odds are you'll be called out again tonight and then where will you be?'

'Exhausted,' Nikki admitted. 'But the exam's only three weeks away, Beattie.'

'And old Doc Maybury told me there's not the least need for you to be sitting the exam yet. He said most doctors wait five years from graduation before even thinking about it, and you've been practising less than that. You'll drive yourself to an early grave, Nikki Russell, you mark my words!'

'Beattie, I'm only twenty-seven.' Nikki smiled placatingly at her housekeeper and pushed stray curls of flaming hair back from her face. 'I'm young and fit. Hard work's not going to kill me.'

'It will if it's all you do.' Beattie sniffed. 'It's no life for a girl, buried here as Eurong's solo GP. You should be out having fun while you're still young. You've a little girl who's growing up without knowing her mother can be fun and happy.' She hesitated. 'Honestly, Nikki, dear, it's been five years since Scott. . .'

Nikki's smile faded and her face closed. 'What I'm doing now has nothing to do with Scott.' She grimaced. 'Or maybe it has. I had fun with Scott. And look where that got me.'

'But——'

'Thanks for the chocolate.' Nikki's eyes told her housekeeper to keep away from the raw spot—the aching pain that had been there for five long years. 'Beattie, I really need to study.'

The housekeeper stared at her young employer in concern. Beattie had known Nikki Russell since childhood and was almost as fond of her as she was of her own family. Nikki's nose was back in her text but Beattie tried one more time.

'While this locum's here,' she started tentatively. 'While he's here, couldn't you get away for a bit? Take Amy and have a few days right away. . .'

'I've employed the locum so I can study,' Nikki said shortly. She shoved her glasses higher on to her nose as she buried her face determinedly in her text. As she did, the front doorbell pealed. 'Damn!' she swore.

'I'll go,' Beattie sighed. 'Oh, my dear, I didn't want you to be called tonight.'

'Leave it, Beattie.' Nikki echoed Beattie's sigh, closed her book and rose. 'You go to bed. I'll deal with it.'

Nikki made her way swiftly through the darkened house to the front door, sending up a silent prayer that whoever was waiting for her had a minor problem. The last thing she needed tonight was major trauma—not when she was so tired.

Still, she might not have a choice. If there was a medical emergency there was only Nikki. On this bleak thought she swung the front door wide—and found herself staring into the most arresting blue eyes she had ever seen.

This was no emergency. The man was standing half turned, as if he had been soaking in the view across the moonlit valley to the sea beyond. There was no panic here.

'Dr Russell?' The man smiled as she frowned across the veranda at him. He held out his hand. 'I'm Luke Marriott.'

Luke Marriott. . . Mechanically Nikki held out her hand and had it enveloped in a much larger one. The stranger's grip was strong and warm, intensely masculine. He stood holding her hand and smiling down at her, and Nikki felt her secure, dull existence shift on its foundations.

She had never seen a man like this. Never. Not even Scott. . .

Good grief! What on earth was she thinking of? Nikki gave herself a mental shake, trying to rid herself of the overwhelming impression of—well, there was no other word for it—of masculinity!

Nikki was tall, but this man was taller by several inches. He was strongly built, with fair, unruly curls that looked in need of a good cut. His face bore two or three days' stubble and his jeans and open-necked shirt were stained with sweat and dust. There was a smudge of dirt across the strong, wide features of his face, and the deep blue eyes laughing down at her in the porch light were creased as though constantly shielded from the sun.

'Luke Marriott. . .' Nikki said blankly.

'Your new locum,' the man explained patiently. 'I know I'm not due until tomorrow but I hitched a lift on a prawn boat rather than wait for the bus.' He grinned ruefully down at himself. 'I hope that explains the dirt—and the smell. I'm not usually so perfumed.'

Nikki wrinkled her nose. Now that he mentioned

it. . .ugh! There was a definite smell of old fish
about him.

'The prawn boat was down in Brisbane for a refit,'
the man explained ruefully. 'One of the deck hands
lives here so I filled his place until we arrived. What
I'd thought would be a great two days' holiday turned
into a solid two nights working.' He looked down to
his grubby sports shoes. 'I hate to think what's on
these,' he grinned. 'I'll take them off before I come
in. That is——' he raised his eyebrows in mock-enquiry
'—if you intend asking me in.'

'I. . .' Nikki shook her head as through trying
to dispel a dream. Luke Marriott. She had advertised
for weeks for a locum and had been so delighted
when this man had rung to accept that she'd asked
little further of him except his registration details.
But. . .

'But we've organised your accommodation at the
hospital,' she stammered. 'There's a room there.'

'There's not,' he told her. 'I've been there and the
night sister's apologetic, but Cook's car's broken down
and if they want Cook on hand for breakfast she stays.
They seemed to think their breakfast is more necessary
than I am—and Cook won't share.'

'But. . .but you can't stay here. . .'

'Look, I only take up six feet of floor space.' The
man's humour was beginning to slip. Clearly he'd
expected a warmer welcome. 'Lady, I've come almost
a thousand miles to do a locum for you. Do you expect
me to find a park bench?'

'I. . .'

'Your night sister said Whispering Palms had at least
six bedrooms and it only held three people. Now, if I
promise to rid myself of prawn bait and berley, and
not indulge in rape or pillage, can Whispering Palms
stretch itself to accommodate me?' The stranger
stepped back as he talked, his eyes following the long
lines of generous verandas with the rows of French

windows opening out to the night breeze. 'Or do you want me to go back to Brisbane?'

Nikki pulled herself together with a visible effort. Of course there was no reason to refuse to accommodate her new locum. If only. . . Well, if only he weren't so. . .

So. . .so she didn't know what! She stood aside and held the door wider.

'Of. . .of course not. Come in, Dr Marriott. Welcome to Eurong.'

'I'm not very,' he said, looking quizzically down at her. What he saw made his deep eyes crease in perplexity. Nikki Russell was a stunner in any man's books. Her fabulous red-gold curls framed an elfin face with huge green eyes which refused to be disguised by her too heavy glasses. She was slender—almost too thin for good health—and her pale skin was shadowed by the traces of exhaustion. The casual jeans and worn cotton shirt she wore accentuated her youth. She looked too young to be a practising doctor. 'And I wonder why not?' he said slowly.

'I'm sorry?' Nikki frowned, trying to make sense of his words.

'You do want a locum?'

'Oh, yes.' Nikki was under control now, moving aside to make way for him. As she did she was intensely conscious of his size—his smell—and it wasn't all fishing-boat smell either. 'It was only that you were so. . . well, unexpected.'

'Because I wasn't due until tomorrow?' he asked.

'Yes,' she said firmly. Why else?

She turned to usher him into the house, but as she did the telephone on the hall table started to ring. Now what? She flashed him a look of apology and went to answer it. It was almost a relief to turn away—to give her confused mind time to settle.

She wasn't granted time. The voice on the other end of the line was harsh and urgent.

'Nikki?' It was Sergeant Milne's voice, Eurong's solitary policeman.

'Yes?' Nikki knew trouble when she heard it. Dan Milne's voice was laced with it.

'You'd better get here fast,' the policeman barked into the phone. 'I've got two kids trapped in a wreck on the beach road and I doubt if either'll make it. They look bloody awful!'

Luke Marriott and a car crash all in one night! Nikki turned from the phone to find her new locum watching her. He'd placed his luggage down on the polished boards of the hall and was listening in concern to Nikki's terse queries.

Behind them, Beattie Gilchrist appeared in her dressing-gown and fluffy slippers. The housekeeper raised her brows in surprise at the strange man making himself at home in the hall, but didn't speak until Nikki put down the phone.

'Trouble?' she said as she saw Nikki's face. What she saw there made her treat the stranger's presence as secondary.

'Beattie, this is Dr Marriott, our new locum,' Nikki said briefly, pushing her hair back in a gesture of exhaustion. 'Can you find him supper and a bed? I have to go. There's a car come off the back beach road and a couple of kids are still inside. Sergeant Milne's there and it looks bad——'

'I don't need supper,' Luke Marriott's deep voice cut across her decisively. He abandoned his battered suitcase and strode back to the door. 'Is the ambulance there?'

'It's on its way. But, look, I can handle——'

'I don't think you can.' The big man was suddenly in control, more assured than Nikki. 'To be honest, you look done in already, and if there are two kids. . . Is there a medic with the ambulance?'

'Our ambulance drivers are volunteers with first-aid certificates,' Nikki admitted. 'But——'

'Then no buts,' the man ordered. 'Let's go, Dr Russell.'

It took five minutes to get to the wrecked car.

Nikki didn't speak but concentrated on the roads, and the man at her side seemed content to let her do so. The local roads were treacherous. The population of Eurong was too small to support major road maintenance and the roads were twisting and narrow.

Above Eurong's swimming beach, the road curved in a sharp U around the headland. The teenagers in the car had tried to take it too fast and a massive eucalyptus had halted their plunge to the sea below.

By the time Nikki's little sedan pulled to a halt at the scene there was a tow-truck and ambulance in attendance, and floodlights lit the wreck from the road above. Nikki left the car and swiftly made her way to the edge of the cliff, abandoning Luke Marriott in her haste. What she saw made her wince with dismay.

The tow-truck driver was securing cables to the rear of the crumpled car. Ernie, the ambulance driver, was half into the wreck and the policeman was behind him. Sergeant Milne looked up and gave a wave that showed real relief as he saw Nikki. He struggled up the cliff to meet her.

'It's bad,' he said briefly, casting a curious glance across at Nikki's companion. 'It's Martin Fleming and Lisa Hay. Lisa's conscious but her legs are crushed between the car and the tree. Martin's unconscious and bleeding like a stuck pig. Ernie's trying to put pressure on now.'

'I'll go down.' Nikki turned to slide down the slope but was stopped by a strong grip on her arm.

'Your bag's in the boot?'

'Yes.' Nikki had forgotten that she wasn't alone. She looked up to Luke Marriott, relief in her eyes. 'If you'll get it. . .'

'There's morphine. . .?'

'There's everything. I. . . We'll need saline. . .'

Luke was already moving. 'That car's stable?' he snapped over his shoulder.

'Now we've secured it, it is.' The policeman grimaced. 'I wouldn't let Ernie in till then. For a while I thought they'd slide right down.'

'We'll need more men to get them out.'

'They're on their way.'

Nikki didn't wait to hear more. She was already sliding.

The car was a mess. The ambulance driver pulled back as Nikki arrived, his face grim and distressed.

'I can't stop the bleeding,' he whispered, his eyes on the conscious girl in the passenger side of the car. Lisa was moaning softly to herself, her body rocking against the savage constriction of her legs. 'And I can't do anything for——'

'Get around to Lisa's side,' Nikki ordered. 'See if you can check those legs for bleeding. And stop her twisting!' She raised her voice, trying to penetrate the girl's pain. 'Lisa, help's here. We'll give you something for the pain while we cut you free. You'll be OK now. Just keep still and let us help you.'

The girl's moans grew louder. She turned wild eyes to Nikki. 'Martin's going to die,' she sobbed. 'And my legs. . . You'll have to cut off my legs. . .'

'No.' Nikki's voice was sharp but she didn't make an impression. She was trying to work as she talked, conscious of the blood pumping through a wound on Martin's scalp. Her fingers searched frantically for the pressure points but her eyes also saw what Lisa was doing to her legs. She was pulling, doing what Nikki could only guess to be more damage.

'I'm going to die. You'll have to cut off my legs. Martin's dead. . .' The girl's voice rose in terrified hysteria and she writhed helplessly against her cruel confinement.

'You're talking nonsense.' A man's clipped, firm voice cut across Lisa's screams. The ambulance driver was edged firmly out of the way and Luke Marriott's face appeared on the other side of the car. His hands came in and caught the hysterical girl's flailing fingers from hauling at her legs. 'Keep still,' he ordered. 'Don't move.' Then, in the fraction of a moment while she reacted to his voice, he produced a syringe, swabbed with lightning speed and plunged the morphine home. 'That's good, Lisa,' he said more gently. 'The pain will ease now and we can cut the metal from your legs.'

'But they're smashed. . .'

'You're cutting them by pulling,' Luke said firmly. 'So don't pull.'

'And Martin's dead. . .'

'Is Martin dead?' Luke looked over to where Nikki had found the point she wanted. Nikki was pushing firmly on a wad of dressing over the wound. At Luke's terse request she looked up.

'No one bleeds this much if they're dead,' she said grimly. 'Ernie, I need a saline drip. If I can replace fluids. . .'

'There you are,' Luke told the frightened girl. He looked down at what he could see of the bottom half of her body. 'Now, if you'll stay absolutely still, I'll see if I can relieve some pressure on your legs.'

It was grim work getting the two from the car, and by the end of it Nikki was despairing for the boy she was treating. Martin was deeply unconscious and the longer he remained unconscious, the worse it looked. The steering-wheel had slammed into his face. He had smashed his cheekbones, but something else was causing the coma. What? She hated to think. All she could do was keep him alive while around them men worked to free them.

Over and over she was grateful for Luke Marriott's presence. What good fairy had brought him to Eurong tonight? Lisa needed attention as much as Martin, and Nikki knew that alone she would have struggled to keep both alive.

Finally the metal panels were ripped from the frame of the car. Martin was freed first. As Nikki, the ambulance driver and the assisting men carefully lifted his unconscious frame on to a stretcher, Nikki turned helplessly to Luke.

'It'll be another ten minutes before we have Lisa free,' Luke told her. 'How far's the hospital?'

'Five minutes.'

'Take him and send the ambulance back for us,' he ordered, and there was nothing Nikki could do but obey.

She didn't have time to think of Luke Marriott for the next half-hour. Nikki didn't have time to do anything but hold desperately to her patient's fragile grip on life. Both she and Martin were fighting, she thought grimly, but only one of them was aware of it.

The nursing staff of Eurong's tiny hospital were out in force—the full complement of five nurses and a ward's maid were all at the hospital before Nikki and her patient reached it. In a tiny community like Eurong, word travelled fast. Everyone knew these two kids, and the nurses were grateful for anything they could do to help.

But there was so little. . . Nikki set up an intravenous infusion, took X-rays and then monitored her patient with an increasing sense of helplessness.

'He's slipping.' Andrea, the hospital charge sister, took Martin's blood-pressure for the twentieth time and looked grimly to where Nikki was adjusting the flow of plasma. 'Isn't there anything we can do?'

'The plane's on its way from Cairns,' Nikki told her. 'It'll be here in an hour. They'll transport him back there.'

'But he's slipping fast.'

'I know.' Nikki looked helplessly down at the boy's pallid face. She suspected what was happening from the X-rays. There was pressure building up in the intracranial cavity. She was faced with an invidious choice—to operate here with her limited skill, or put the boy on the plane, knowing that by the time the plane landed in Cairns he'd probably be dead. 'I can't operate,' she whispered. 'I haven't the skills. . .'

There was so much to this job. She would never be skilful enough to cope with the demands on her. Nikki had done obstetrics, basic surgery and anaesthetics but now—now she wanted a competent neurosurgeon right here and now. And because she hadn't done the training this boy would die.

'I can.' The voice sounded behind her and Nikki spun around. Luke Marriott had quietly entered the theatre and was standing watching her.

He looked more disreputable than he had when she'd first seen him. The travel stains and the marks from catching prawns for two nights had been augmented by an hour trying to free the injured girl. His shirt was ripped and blood-stained. Even his fair hair was filthy, matted with dirt and blood. 'Intracranial bleed?' he asked.

'Yes.'

'I've stabilised Lisa,' he said briefly. 'She'll make it. She has two broken legs but they'll wait for surgery in Cairns. She's out to it now. If you prep, Dr Russell, I'll throw myself through the shower, scrub and operate here.' He turned to the junior nurse. 'Show me where to go. Fast.'

'But you can't,' Nikki said blankly.

'Why not?' The fair-haired man turned back to her and his eyes seemed suddenly older than Nikki had thought. Despite the dirt, he looked hard, professional and totally in control. 'You're wasting time, Dr Russell. Prep, please, and fast.'

'But you're not——'

'I'm a surgeon,' he snapped. 'And I've done enough neurology to get me through. Now move!'

Nikki moved.

The burr hole was the work of an expert. Nikki could only watch and marvel, in the few fleeting moments she could spare from her concentration on the anaesthetic. Luke Marriott's fingers were skilled and sure. It was Martin's good fairy that had sent him here tonight.

What on earth was such a man doing as a relieving locum in a place like Eurong? Luke Marriott's skills belonged in a large city teaching hospital. For him to be volunteering to work for the meagre wage of a locum for three weeks. . .

There was little time for her to question his motives. All Nikki's energy had to focus on the job she was doing. Skilled surgery such as Luke Marriot was performing took every ounce of her anaesthetic skill, and she knew that the nurses too were being pushed to their limits. At one stage she raised her eyes to meet the eyes of her charge nurse. Andrea pursed her lips in a silent whistle of wonder, and Nikki agreed with her totally.

And then, finally, this strange surgeon was done. He dressed the site with care and signalled for Nikki to reverse the anaesthetic.

'We've done all we can,' he said grimly. 'Now it's up to Martin.'

'His parents are outside.' Nikki was still fiercely concentrating. She wasn't going to slip now, when Luke's part had been so expertly played.

'I'll take over the anaesthetic,' Luke Marriot told her, his voice gentling. This was the job all medicos hated—to face parents when they couldn't totally reassure. 'You know them, Nikki?'

Nikki nodded numbly. She stayed where she was until Luke reached her and his fingers took the intubation tube. As they did, their hands touched and

Nikki felt a flash of warmth that jolted her. That, and the gentleness of his eyes. . . He understood what she was facing, and that, on its own, made her job easier.

'I'll go,' she whispered, and left him with his patient.

The few moments with the two sets of parents were as bad as they could be. Nikki tried her best to reassure them. This sort of thing hadn't been so bad before she had Amy, she reflected sadly, but now. . . How would she feel if someone were telling her these things about her lovely daughter?

'We're taking them both down to Cairns,' she told them gently. 'We can take you on the plane but you must be back here in twenty minutes with what you need. Overnight gear for yourselves and a few things Martin and Lisa will want. The hospital will provide the necessities but a few personal belongings make a difference.' She hesitated. 'Maybe a few of Martin's favourite tapes. He may. . .he may be in a coma for a while. Sound is important.'

Martin's dad's eyes filled with tears. 'A coma. . .for a while. . . How the hell long?' he demanded roughly.

'I don't know,' Nikki said honestly. 'Dr Marriott has lifted the pressure but there may have been damage done before that. We can only wait.'

Luke was waiting for her as she returned to Theatre. 'Bad?' he said softly, and Nikki looked up at him. For some stupid reason she felt like weeping. This wasn't Nikki Russell—professional—untouchable.

'Terrific,' she said sarcastically, and her tone was harder than she intended. 'What do you think?'

His face tightened and he turned to the sink. 'Sorry I asked.'

Nikki bit her lip. She followed him across and mechanically started to wash.

'You'll fly to Cairns with them?' she asked tentatively. Normally it would be her making the long flight, and she hated the flights with emergency patients. It left Eurong with no doctor within thirty miles. Still, both Lisa and Martin needed a doctor on the trip, and now there was Luke Marriott ready to go.

Or maybe not. Luke shook his head. 'Your job, Dr Russell.'

Nikki stared at him. 'But if something goes wrong. . . It's you who has the neurology skills, Dr Marriott.'

'And a fat lot of good they'll do me at ten thousand feet. You can take blood-pressure and fix a drip just as well as I can, Dr Russell.' They were being abruptly formal and all of a sudden it sounded absurd. The trough where they were washing was meant for one doctor. They were confined in too small a space and the night was too hot for comfort. The nurses had turned on the air-conditioning but it was still making a half-hearted effort to cool.

'But. . .' Nikki tried again. 'But I've a little girl at home.'

'You've a daughter?' His brows rose as if the news shocked him. Nikki winced, wishing for the thousandth time she looked her age.

'I have,' she told him. 'Amy's four and she worries.'

'But your housekeeper is there.'

'Yes. But——'

'And I'll be there too.' He smiled, and his smile held a trace of self-mockery. 'I'm held to be good with children.'

'But——'

He shook his head and his hands came up suddenly to grip her shoulders. 'Dr Russell, do you know what I'm wearing at this particular moment?'

Nikki stared. His deep eyes were challenging her, and behind the challenge was the hint of laughter.

'I don't know. . .' Nikki looked down, writhing in the unaccustomed hold. She didn't enjoy being so close. Then she gasped. Luke Marriott was wearing a theatre gown. Nothing else. Below the gown hard, muscled legs emerged—naked. Even his feet were bare.

'I'm in my birthday suit,' he grinned. 'Without my theatre gown I'm really something.' His smile deepened, and he released her to turn his back, so that the ties behind him faced her. 'Want to untie me and check it out?'

'No!' Nikki stepped back in horror. He turned back and smiled.

'Well, I'm sure as hell not wearing an operating gown all the way to Cairns. My stuff was caked with dirt. I couldn't wear it in Theatre. And these gowns are meant to fit someone about six inches shorter than I am. Sister's already told me you keep a change of clothes here, Dr Russell. On the grounds that you'd look better in your change of clothes than I would, you're going to Cairns.'

'But——'

He sighed, leaned back and folded his arms. 'What's the matter, Dr Russell? Aren't you happy leaving Eurong and your daughter to my tender mercies? Don't you trust me?'

Nikki stared up at him. The deep blue eyes mocked her with their trace of laughter.

For the life of her, she couldn't answer.

CHAPTER TWO

MARTIN recovered consciousness before the plane touched down at Cairns.

For Nikki it was a weird journey. She felt as if she had been snatched from her nice, safe existence, and only part of that feeling was due to flying to Cairns. She watched over her patients while she tried hard to avoid thinking of Luke Marriott.

'He's nice, isn't he?' Lisa whispered as she stirred from her drugged sleep and found the strength to speak.

'Who?' Nikki asked. She knew already whom Lisa was talking about.

'The new doctor. He. . .he saved my life.'

Nikki shook her head, but part of her acknowledged the truth of Lisa's words. His presence might not have saved Lisa's life but it had probably spared her legs, and as for the boy she was with. . .

Nikki checked Martin for the hundredth time and noticed with satisfaction the lessening of his unconsciousness. He stirred just as they touched down, his eyes flickering open and gazing upwards in dazed confusion.

'You're safe,' Nikki told him gently. 'You and Lisa crashed the car. Lisa's here with you. She's OK. We're taking you both to hospital.'

It was all he could cope with hearing. His eyelids lowered and he slept.

At Cairns Nikki was suddenly redundant. Forewarned, there were ambulances and doctors waiting as their flight landed. Martin's condition was less serious now than they had feared, so Nikki could slip into the background. She was content to do so. By now the

cumulative effects of two sleepless nights were showing. It was five in the morning and she was close to
exhaustion.

Someone showed her to a sparsely furnished room
at the hospital. All Nikki saw was the bed. Somehow
she shed her clothes, slipped between cool sheets, and
seconds later was asleep.

Nikki woke to heat. There was a big ceiling fan in the
bedroom but she'd been too tired to think of turning
it on. Now the temperature in the room had risen to
the point of discomfort. Nikki opened her eyes, looked
automatically at the wristwatch on her arm and sat up
with a start. Midday.

Midday! It couldn't be. She stared again and shook
her wrist. The daily flight up to Cooktown—her only
means of getting home—left at eleven a.m. Now. . .
now she was stuck here for another twenty-four hours
whether she liked it or not.

She flung back her sheet in distress. Someone should
have woken her. They knew the routine. The staff here
knew she had a flight to catch. Then a knock on the
door made her dive back for the modesty of her bed-
clothes. The door opened and a smiling face appeared.
It was Miss Charlotte Cain, a young surgeon whose
friendship with Nikki dated from medical school.

'Hi, Nikki,' Charlotte smiled. 'Welcome to the day.'
The white-coated young doctor looked down at her
watch and her smile widened. 'I can't say good morning
any more, that's for sure.'

'Charlie, what on earth were you doing letting me
sleep?' Nikki demanded angrily. 'You knew I had a
plane to catch.'

'I'm only following orders,' Charlotte grinned. 'I
hardly dared do anything else.'

'What do you mean?'

'Just that Luke Marriott rang from Eurong early this
morning,' she told the bemused Nikki. 'He rang to

find out how his patients were—*his* patients, mind—
I think you've suffered an insurrection in your absence.
When we reassured him as to Martin and Lisa's condition, he turned his attention to you. He said you
weren't to be woken. He told us he didn't expect you
back in Eurong until tomorrow. We are to pass on
instructions to you to get some rest. Go shopping, the
man said. I am informed everything is under control
at Eurong and you are not required. An autocratic
male, is our Mr Marriott. Not a man to deny, I'd say.'
Charlotte sat down on the bed, raised her eyebrows
at her friend and grinned. She had the look of someone
who was enjoying herself hugely.

'Mr Marriott. . .' Nikki stared up at Charlotte in
confusion. 'So the man really is a surgeon?'

'One of the best,' Charlotte said simply. 'As your
young Martin can testify. He's fully conscious and
showing no signs of permanent damage.' Charlotte
shook her head. 'I wish I could operate like that.'

'I don't understand.' Nikki folded her sheet more
closely about her and stared up at her friend.

'What don't you understand?'

'Anything,' Nikki wailed. 'But especially I don't
understand why someone with Luke Marriott's skill
and training accepts the job as my locum. It doesn't
make sense.' She looked desperately at her friend.
'Make sense of it for me, Charlie?'

Charlotte shook her dark hair. 'I can't,' she admitted. 'We were all amazed when you contacted us last
night and told us who was operating. Luke Marriott
resigned from this place two years ago. We thought
he'd gone overseas but no one heard. And then he
springs up with you in Eurong—in the nick of time,
as far as I can gather.'

In the nick of time. . . It had certainly been that.
But why?

'Did anything happen?' Nikki asked slowly. 'I mean,
why did he leave here to do locum work?'

'Who knows?'

'There must be something,' Nikki frowned. 'Did something dreadful happen? Was there a lawsuit or medical mistake that would make him give up surgery?'

'Didn't you ask for details of his past when you employed him?' Charlotte asked, amused. 'Surely an outstanding lawsuit would have to appear on his curriculum vitae?'

'I didn't ask for his curriculum vitae,' Nikki snapped, and then at the look on her friend's face she changed her tone. 'I checked he was currently registered and left it at that. Honestly, Charlotte, I was just so tired I thought anyone would do, as long as they were qualified and registered. I mean, I wasn't going to leave the town.'

'You mean you were going to do your usual trick of employing a locum and then doing the work yourself,' Charlotte said drily. 'For heaven's sake, Nikki——'

'Leave it, Charlie,' Nikki said brusquely. She looked up, saw the fleeting look of hurt in her friend's eyes and immediately regretted her words. 'Look, Charlie, it's just that. . .'

'It's just that if you stop working then you have time to think,' her friend retorted. And then a sudden smile flashed over her face. 'Well, you and Luke Marriott should get on famously. Two workaholics and only enough work for one. Dear, oh, dear. . .'

'So tell me about him,' Nikki demanded, anxious to get the conversation away from herself. 'Why on earth is he acting as a locum if he's so darned clever and conscientious? He looks like. . .' She thought back to Luke Marriott's disreputable appearance, and the sudden memory of naked legs appearing from under his scanty hospital gown made her almost gasp. 'He looks like a bum to me,' she said unsteadily.

'Well, he's not a bum.' Charlotte shook her head vehemently, frowning. 'I suppose we're talking of the same Luke Marriott? I don't think I've ever seen the man without imported, tailored suits and amazingly expensive silk ties.' She looked at Nikki. 'What's your Luke Marriott like?'

How to describe naked legs and laughing blue eyes. . .? Nikki couldn't. She opened her mouth and tried but the words stuck. And then Charlotte laughed.

'OK,' she smiled. 'That's our Luke you're thinking of. I know Luke Marriott. There's not many men who could make you look like that, Nikki Russell, but Luke Marriott has to be a good bet. He hasn't changed, then.'

'Hasn't changed. . .?'

'Luke Marriott was the most gorgeous male within jet-plane distance of this hospital,' Charlotte said firmly. 'He had every junior nurse, some senior ones, and a few female doctors besides, making fools of themselves every time he walked past. He's broken more hearts than I care to name.' She peered at Nikki. 'Not yours yet, sweetie?'

'Don't be ridiculous,' Nikki snapped, and to her annoyance found herself flushing.

'No.' Charlotte stood up abruptly. 'I'm not being ridiculous. Nikki, it's five years since Scott——'

'I don't want to talk about Scott.'

'I know,' her friend said grimly. 'You don't want to remember Scott. Well, that's never going to happen if you don't ease up on work and start enjoying yourself a bit more,' Charlotte said bluntly. She looked at her watch. 'Hey, your new locum ordered you to shop,' she smiled. 'And I have the afternoon off. When was the last time you went clothes shopping, Dr Russell?'

'I don't need clothes,' Nikki snapped. 'I can use this afternoon at the library. I need to study, Charlie.'

'The medical library is closed on Wednesday afternoons,' her friend grinned. 'Now isn't that a shame? And you haven't a text with you—and I'm damned if I'll lend you a single one of mine.'

'Charlie——'

'Nikki Russell, you must have more money than you
know what to do with. Your parents left you that
fabulous house, and you have a perfectly sound income
from a too busy medical practice. And I don't see a
single sign of frivolous spending. Those jeans you were
wearing last night were years old. Now either you come
shopping with me or I'll personally ring the airport
and cancel your flight home tomorrow.' She put her
hands on her hips. 'Coming, Dr Russell?'

Nikki sighed. Well, maybe she could do with some
new jeans. . . 'If you're not doing anything. . .' she
said reluctantly.

'I'm doing something all right,' her friend grinned.
'I'm spending the afternoon with my closest friend to
spend someone else's money. There's nothing I could
enjoy more.'

'I have to telephone Amy.'

'There's a telephone beside your bed,' her friend
told her. 'You have fifteen minutes, Dr Russell. And
then you're coming shopping, whether you like it
or not.'

Jeans weren't what Charlotte envisaged when she
said shopping. Charlie dragged her friend from one
shop to another and there wasn't a pair of jeans in
sight.

'Honestly, Charlie,' Nikki expostulated. 'This stuff
is crazy.' The shop Charlie had pushed her into was
up-market and exclusive, dealing in everything from
beautiful imported shoes and designer fashions to the
most indulgent of lingerie. Nikki fingered the soft Swiss
cotton of the dress her friend had just discovered. The
frock was lovely, light and soft, with swirling green
pastels which lit the brilliant red of Nikki's hair. 'I
wouldn't wear this in Eurong. It'd be wasted.'

'Maybe yesterday you wouldn't have worn it,' her
friend grinned. 'But today. . .today Luke Marriott is
your new locum. I wouldn't be seen dead in anything

less than this dress if Luke Marriott was in the vicinity.
Honest, Nikki——'

'Charlie, I am not the least bit interested in Luke
Marriott,' Nikki snapped.

'You're lying,' Charlotte said simply. 'My grand-
mother would look twice at Luke Marriott. And she's
been happily married to my grandfather for fifty years!'

'Charlie——'

'Look, just try it on,' Charlie pleaded. She thrust
the dress into Nikki's hands and pushed her towards
a changing-room. 'You could even wear this to work
—with a nice white coat over the top. It's time you
gave the bachelors of Eurong their money's worth. I
bet you charge top rates even when you wear your
mouldy old jeans.'

Half laughing, half exasperated, Nikki gave in. She
was fond of Charlie—in fact Charlotte Cain had been
a true friend for a long time. It wouldn't hurt to
humour her. And these clothes—she fingered the soft
cotton with a trace of regret—these clothes could join
the rest of the things she had put away five years ago.
Her mother's jewellery. Her cosmetics. Her contact
lenses. She looked up to her face and grimaced at
the too heavy glasses. She knew she was being stupid
wearing these but they were a defence against something she no longer wanted.

They were a defence against the likes of Luke
Marriott. Unbidden, the thought of Nikki's new locum
flashed before her and it was all she could do not to
rip the dress she was trying on from her back. The
thought of him produced something that was close
to panic.

This was crazy. There was no need for her to panic.
Luke Marriott obviously had problems of his own and
a three-week stint as her locum was hardly going to
change either of them. Her panic was inexplicable and
needless.

Nikki forced herself to concentrate on the dress. It

was pretty, there was no doubting that. It fell in soft folds around her slim form, catching the colour of her eyes and highlighting her brilliant hair. She should get her hair cut, she thought crossly. There was too much of it. Or maybe she should just tie it back into a severe knot. She shoved her glasses back on and opened the curtain. Charlie and the shop assistant were both waiting.

'Oh, Nikki, it's lovely!' Charlie exclaimed delightedly. 'Don't you like it?'

'It's OK,' Nikki agreed reluctantly. She fingered the fine cotton. 'It feels good.'

'And so it should.' Charlotte took her by the shoulders and spun her around. 'It really makes you look like. . .well, like you ought to look. Apart from those glasses.'

'There's nothing wrong with my glasses.'

'Why do you wear them all the time?' Charlotte demanded. 'You know you only need them for reading.'

'I'm more comfortable with them on.'

'But you used to wear contact lenses.'

'Well, I don't any more,' Nikki snapped. 'I'll take this off.'

'You'll buy it?'

'If you think I ought to,' Nikki said flatly.

The shop assistant had been watching the proceedings with interest. 'It does look pretty,' she said. 'But have a look at it in the full-length mirror before you buy it. There's one just around the corner here.'

'I don't need to.'

'Yes, you do,' Charlotte said, her voice firm. 'Go and look, Nikki.' Then she reached forward towards the objects on Nikki's nose. 'And look without these awful glasses!'

'Charlie——'

'Can you see without them?' Charlotte demanded.

'Yes, but——'

'Then look without them.' Charlotte firmly removed the offending articles and thrust her forward. 'Now go and look at what you should be, Nikki Russell!'

Nikki was propelled firmly forward by the shop assistant. The assistant had obviously taken Nikki's lack of interest as a personal challenge. She stood next to Nikki, chatting cheerfully at Nikki's image in the mirror.

'It looks so good, miss. You should wear that colour all the time. Green really suits you.' She smiled up at her reluctant client. 'And your friend's right. You shouldn't wear those glasses.'

Nikki stared at her reflection and a part of her cringed. She wanted no part of this. To be beautiful. . . Scott had told her she was beautiful. . .

'I'll get changed now,' she said firmly.

'You will take it?' the assistant said anxiously.

'Oh, yes.' Nikki grimaced. Charlotte would give her no peace unless she did, and her friendship with Charlotte was important. Speaking of Charlotte. . . She looked around. Where was her friend?

'Charlie?'

'Your friend must have slipped out.' The assistant frowned. She looked around the shop, visions of shop-lifting clearly flashing through her mind. People who distracted the shop assistant and left were a worry. Surely not. These two women seemed. . .well, classy.

But Charlotte had gone.

And then Nikki parted the curtain to her changing-cubicle and realised with horror that something else had gone as well. All her clothes. Everything. Her sandals. Even her glasses. . .

The shop assistant was right behind her. Seeing what Nikki had seen, she gave a nervous but relieved giggle. 'Oh, dear,' she offered. 'Your friend seems to have. . . to have taken all your clothes.'

'Charlie. . .' Nikki's voice was an angry wail. What on earth was her friend playing at?

'I'm back.' It was the cheerful voice of Charlotte coming back in the door from the street. 'Missed me?'

'Charlie, where are my clothes?' Nikki asked softly. Her tone was low and dangerous.

Charlie grinned, unperturbed.

'I put 'em in a rubbish bin,' she confessed blithely. 'Actually I put 'em in about five garbage bins. I put your jeans in one. I put your shirt in another. One sandal per bin. I wish I'd been able to get your knickers and bra. But you will be sensible and buy some more of those, won't you, sweetie?'

'Charlotte!'

'Well, you were going to buy new clothes,' her friend said innocently. 'You said you were. And you'd never choose to wear those old things when you have lovely new clothes, now would you?' Her face assumed an expression of innocence. 'You weren't buying these just to humour me, now were you, Nikki?'

It was so close to the truth that Nikki gasped. She opened her mouth to say something and then couldn't think of a thing to say. Finally she closed her mouth again and contented herself with glaring.

'That's better,' Charlie said. She turned to the shop assistant. 'You know, this girl has nothing now but the clothes she's standing in. I think we need at least a couple more outfits.'

The sales assistant choked on shocked laughter. 'Oh, yes, miss,' she breathed. She turned to Nikki. 'We have the loveliest linen suit that you'd look smashing in.'

'Wheel it out,' Charlie said firmly.

'Charlotte, where are my glasses?' Nikki said awfully, and her friend threw up her hands in mock-fright.

'Beats me,' she laughed. 'Either Mall Litter Bin 36 or Mall Litter Bin 39. Or was that your left sandal?' She shrugged.

'Charlie. . .'

Her friend put her hands on her hips. 'Nikki Russell,

you are my very best friend.' She smiled, then her face
grew suddenly serious. 'You have been vegetating in
Eurong for the past five years with no one to appreciate
how lovely you really are. Now I find that one of the
most eligible males I know is working as your locum.
I'm damned if I'll let you go home wearing those
glasses. I'd be failing in my friendship if I did. Now
try this suit on, Nikki Russell, and let's have no more
nonsense.'

'Charlie, I am not the least interested in Luke
Marriott.' It was almost a wail.

'Well, that's fine,' her friend said simply. 'All I'm
ensuring is that Luke Marriott is interested in you.'

It was a still angry Dr Russell who climbed from the
plane at Eurong airstrip the next day. The wind was
hot and blustery. The dress Charlotte had chosen hung
coolly on Nikki's slim body, fluttering in the breeze.
It felt soft, pleasant and frightening. Nikki's legs were
bare apart from simple crystal-green sandals. Her hair
wisped around her face, no longer held back by the
rigid frames of her glasses. Nikki's fingers kept moving
self-consciously to her face, but there was no dark
shield to hide her. She felt strange, and frighteningly
exposed.

'It's only until I reach home,' she muttered to herself. 'I can change immediately.' If only she had more
glasses. . .

The pilot had come around to help her from the
cabin. As she thanked him he reached down on to
the floor and retrieved a package the size of a small
suitcase.

'This is for you too, Doc,' he grinned. 'A Miss Cain
sent it out to the airport last night. Said we weren't
to give it to you until now.'

Nikki looked down at the package and her lips tightened. The package was emblazoned with the logo of
the shop she had visited the day before. She had

refused to buy anything more than the dress she was wearing, but she knew already what would be in the parcel. Everything Charlotte had pleaded with her to buy, she imagined.

'I suppose these are all paid for,' she said icily, and the pilot grinned as though he too was in on the plot.

'They're bought on approval,' he said.

'Well, here.' Nikki thrust the package at him. 'I don't approve. You can take them right back.'

'Not me, Doc.' The pilot backed off with his hands held up in negation. 'I promised Miss Cain that they'd stay in Eurong for a least a week. If you don't want them after that, she says I can bring 'em back.'

'But——'

'You wouldn't have me break a promise,' he smiled.

'Yes.' Nikki put the parcel down on the tarmac and glared.

His grin deepened and he shook his head in mock-sorrow. 'Tut-tut. What a thing to say. Now, I'm sorry, Doctor, but undermining my moral values is something I don't hold with. Have it here in a week if you want it returned.'

'Fine,' Nikki snapped. 'I will.'

'Now, Doc. . .' Pete was looking anxious and Nikki sighed and relented. It was no fault of the pilot's that she had such a scheming friend.

'Sorry, Pete. It's just that I'm feeling managed.'

'Yeah, she looks managing, that Miss Cain.' The pilot looked behind her across the runway. 'And speaking of managing. . .is this your new locum?'

Nikki spun around. She'd been expecting Beattie to meet her, but striding across the tarmac was Dr Luke Marriott. He was walking swiftly towards them, carrying a parcel in his arms.

It was all Nikki could do not to gasp. The change in the man was extraordinary. Instead of the disreputable vagrant of two days ago, this man was well-dressed, arrogant and assured. It showed in his stride, in his immaculately tailored linen trousers and quality open-necked shirt—and in the way his eyes dropped approvingly over Nikki's figure.

'Well, well, well.' He whistled soundlessly as he neared them. 'A veritable transformation. . .'

'You should talk,' Nikki said abruptly, and then flushed. Her eyes fell away. She didn't know how to react to this man.

He grinned. 'Didn't you like my coating of prawns, bait and blood?' he smiled. He looked up to the pilot. 'Thanks for bringing her back.'

It was as if he were a parent thanking the air hostess for looking after a child. Nikki's flush deepened and she felt anger mounting within her.

'Couldn't Beattie come to collect me?' she asked ungraciously.

'You don't approve of the substitute?' he demanded, his eyes still laughing. He motioned down to the parcel in his arms. 'Beattie and Amy are involved in a most important function at Amy's kindergarten. They said they'd meet you at home. Speaking of Beattie, she asked me to send this down to Cairns.' He handed it over to the pilot. 'Can I leave it with you? The address is on the label.' Then he turned back to Nikki. 'Shall we go?'

'Fine.' Nikki turned away but the pilot stopped her.

'You've forgotten your parcel, Doc,' he said apologetically, looking down at the bulky package still at Nikki's feet. He looked from Luke to Nikki, obviously relishing the undercurrents he was sensing.

'Leave it here until next week,' Nikki snapped. 'I don't want it.'

'I'm not doing that,' the pilot said definitely. 'This building is open to heaven knows who. You'll have to take it.' He turned to Luke. 'Can you take it for Doc Russell?'

Luke nodded and held out his hands to accept it. 'I

get rid of one and I'm given another. What is it?' he asked curiously.

'I gather our Doc Russell went shopping yesterday,' the pilot grinned.

'As per instructions.' Luke Marriott smiled and the smile made Nikki's heart give a sickening lurch. 'Very good, Dr Russell. I'm glad to see you can follow orders.'

'Excuse me,' Nikki said icily. 'I thought I was the general practitioner and you were the locum. Or was I mistaken? Since when has the locum given orders to his employer?'

Luke's smile only deepened. 'For three weeks, you said, I was the general practitioner and you were out of work,' he told her. 'And that's the way it's going to be.'

'Over my dead body,' Nikki said savagely; and then wished she hadn't. Both Luke and the pilot obviously found it enormously amusing.

'Come on, Nikki Russell,' Luke Marriott said kindly, in the voice of one humouring a fractious child. 'Let's take you home.'

'Dr Marriott. . .'

'It's Mr Marriott,' Luke told her. 'I thought your friends in Cairns would have told you that. But you can call me Luke if you like.'

Nikki stood almost speechless. The ground was being swept from beneath her feet. She felt as if every foundation she possessed was cracking. 'Luke Marriott, I don't know what the hell you're playing at. . .' she started.

'I'm not playing at all.' Luke raised his free hand in acknowledgement and farewell to the pilot, tucked Nikki's parcel under his arm and started walking towards the hangars. In the distance Nikki saw her car parked, waiting. He glanced at his watch. 'In fact, I'm late.'

'Late?'

'For afternoon surgery,' he informed her blandly. 'I have patients booked.'

'My patients!'

'No.' He shook his head. 'They're mine. You're not wanted for three weeks, Dr Russell. You can take yourself off to your texts or sleep by the swimming-pool for all I care. But you're not working.'

'But——'

'Beattie has explained things to me,' Luke went on blandly. 'She tells me you're set on passing this exam and it's my responsibility to see that you do. And I'm one to take my responsibilities very seriously.'

'I'm not your responsibility. . .'

'No. But your practice is. For the next three weeks, Dr Russell, you are not wanted.'

CHAPTER THREE

'WELL, we think he's lovely.'

Nikki's housekeeper and her small daughter were smitten. Beattie stood at the big wooden table, mechanically mixing her dough, her eyes far-away. Amy was fixed on her mother's lap, her small fingers fingering the soft fabric of Nikki's dress in blatant admiration. 'Oh, Nikki, he's just the best thing. . .' Beattie continued dreamily.

'Since sliced bread,' Nikki snapped. She was perched on the stool as she held her daughter, sipping tea and feeling stranger and stranger. It was mid-afternoon. Her surgery was crowded, she knew, and she wasn't even welcome there, much less wanted.

'If you come near the place then I'll pick you up and deposit you outside on your very neat bottom,' Luke Marriott had said sternly, and by the look in his eyes Nikki wasn't going to test the truth of his statement. She had the feeling that Luke Marriott didn't make idle threats.

'But what's he doing here?' Nikki asked for the fiftieth time. 'He's a surgeon, for heaven's sake. What's he doing acting as temporary locum in Eurong?'

'I have no idea,' Beattie said, giving her dough a sound pummelling. 'All I know is that's he's an answer to a prayer, Nikki Russell, and you don't ask questions when fate plays you lucky.'

'He might be the answer to your prayers,' Nikki said bitterly, 'but he's not the answer to mine. A more autocratic, overbearing. . .'

'I know,' Beattie sighed. 'Isn't it lovely?'

'Beattie!'

'I don't mean he's rude,' Beattie said, shocked by

35

Nikki's tone. 'He just knows what has to be done.'
She looked down at her pastry. 'And he really likes
my cooking.' She cast a look of disapproval at her
employer. 'No just picking around the edges. I asked
him what he'd like for dinner tonight and he said, "The
same as last night—only more!" I won't give it to him,
of course. Last night I made a chicken casserole but
tonight I'll do a standing rib roast with Yorkshire pud-
ding—and have apple pie to follow. Eh, but it's good
to cook for a man again. I haven't since my John died.'

'But he's not staying here,' Nikki said, frowning.
'Isn't he supposed to be staying at the hospital? I'd
arranged it.'

'I know.' Beattie eyed her employer doubtfully. 'The
thing is, Matron rang while you were in Cairns and
asked if we could have him stay on for a while longer.
Cook's done the cylinder-head on her car and it'll be
a week or more before they can get the part. Mean-
while she'll have to stay at the hospital—and Matron
doesn't want to use a ward.' Beattie took a deep breath
and her dubious look intensified. 'So. . .so I told her
of course we'd have him here.'

'Beattie!'

'We've plenty of room,' her housekeeper told her
severely. 'For heaven's sake, Nikki, there are three
spare bedrooms. You hardly have to see the man apart
from mealtimes.'

'I'll have my meals in my study,' Nikki said angrily
and Beattie smiled. 'With Amy.'

'Mummy, why don't you like him?' Amy had been
intent on her drink and biscuits. Finished with the
serious business of life, she turned to her mother. 'We
think he's nice. And he makes us laugh.' She frowned
direfully at her mother. 'I'm not eating in the study if
Dr Luke's in the dining-room.'

'Dr Luke!' Nikki frowned back down at her daughter. 'Mr Marriott to you.'

'He said I could call him Dr Luke,' Amy announced,

'I said no one would think he was proper if we called him Mister, and he thanked me for the advice. And he agrees. And I showed him the swimming-pool this morning and he said he'd teach me to dog-paddle. Starting tomorrow. So he has to stay here.'

'Well, there you are, then,' Beattie grinned. Her smile faded a little and she looked down at Nikki in concern. 'It's better this way,' she said gently. 'The night calls come here and you'd be going out anyway if he was staying down at the hospital. This way. . .'

'I know.' Nikki threw up her hands. 'This way I have nothing to do except study.'

'Which is what you wanted, isn't it?' Beattie said doubtfully, and Nikki gave a reluctant smile.

'Yes, Beattie,' she said slowly. 'It's what I wanted.'

Nikki left and made her way back to her study. Her text still stood open at the causes of renal failure. Nikki picked it up and frowned at the blurred image. She'd have to put in her contact lenses and part of her didn't want to.

She put a hand up to her face in a gesture of distress. Her heavy glasses were a token of her defence against the world, but they were a comfort to her. Charlotte had thought she was doing her friend a favour depriving her of them. If she had known how distressed it was making Nikki feel. . .

'How exposed, you mean,' Nikki whispered, and then shook her head angrily. She wasn't exposed. There wasn't the slightest reason to believe that Luke Marriott was the least bit interested in her. 'I can wear what I like,' Nikki muttered, looking down uneasily at the attractive dress she was wearing. Still. . .

Still, she would just go and change before Luke Marriott came home for dinner. After all, she had to go to her bedroom to find her contact lenses anyway. . .

Two minutes later she was back in the kitchen.

'Beattie, where are the rest of my jeans?' she asked softly. The housekeeper looked up, startled, from her cooking and turned a becoming shade of pink.

'Oh, Nikki, dear, you startled me. . .'

'Beattie, where are my jeans?' Nikki's voice was dangerously quiet. She stood with her hands linked behind her, staring at the elderly Beattie.

'All of them?' Beattie asked. She sounded flustered.

'All of them.'

'Well, I sent them to Charlotte, of course.' Beattie's expression of innocence didn't quite come off. 'Like she asked me to.'

'Beattie——'

'Now, I know you'll think we're interfering,' Beattie said, paying minute attention to the pastry she was crimping, 'but Miss Charlotte rang and said you'd bought the most lovely clothes and you wouldn't be game to wear them if you didn't get some encouragement.' She flushed even redder. 'So she told me to burn them. And I wouldn't, of course,' she said virtuously as she saw Nikki's jaw drop. 'So then she told me to pack them all up and put them on the aeroplane back down to Cairns. Said she'd look after them until you wanted them again.'

'So. . .' Nikki stared, speechless.

'So I did. I asked your new locum to give them to the pilot when he met you from the plane.'

'Beattie——'

'And Miss Charlotte said you were to yell at her and not me.' And then Beattie smiled a cheeky smile. 'But you can yell at me if you like. My shoulders are broad enough to take it.' She left what she was doing, folded her floury arms and fixed her young employer with a hard stare. 'Miss Charlotte thinks it's time you started living again and I'm not disagreeing.'

Nikki sank on to a kitchen chair. Her anger was palpable. 'So you take my clothes. . .'

'Those things weren't clothes,' Beattie said harshly. 'They were a disguise, is what Miss Charlotte reckoned, and she's right. You're pretty as any girl in

Eurong, Nikki Russell, and you're too darned young
to be as bitter and reclusive as you've been.' She sniffed
defensively. 'So we've taken a hand.' She buried her
hands in her pastry again. 'And if you don't like it you
can sack me, but I've done no more than my Christian
duty or what your mum would have done if she'd been
alive.' She sniffed again. 'I was that fond of your
mother! And I've a duty to her too——'

The telephone broke across her words. It was just as
well, Nikki thought grimly. In another minute Beattie
would be in tears. Flashing a look of frustrated fury
at her housekeeper, she crossed to the bench to answer
it. It was the last person she wanted to speak to. Luke
Marriott. . .

'OK, I said I wouldn't disturb you.' From the other
end of the line his voice was clipped and efficient. 'But
I've a child here I'm unhappy about. Karen Mears.'

Karen. . . Nikki's anger was placed aside. 'What is
it?' she asked quietly.

'It's a greenstick fracture of her arm. But am I right
in worrying?'

Nikki sighed. 'Yeah,' she said grimly. 'We'll have
to get her to hospital. I'll be right there.'

'No.' The voice was firm and authoritative. 'I just
wanted my suspicions confirmed. I can deal with it.'

'But Mrs Mears will never let you——'

'She'll let me.'

'Luke, Mrs Mears has problems. . .'

'None that justifies this. Her problems can wait. For
now, all we need to do is make sure Karen's protected.
Then we act.'

'But——'

'Nikki, I don't need you. Go back to your study.
I'll see you tonight.' The line went dead. Nikki was
left holding the useless telephone. She stared down.
Karen. . .

At least this showed that Luke Marriott was thinking as he worked. Most children presenting with a

greenstick fracture would not excite attention. Karen, though. . .

Karen was eight years old—the eldest of a family of four children. Her father had walked out a year ago, and Nikki was sure Mrs Mears wasn't coping. Karen seemed to be bearing the brunt of it. She'd been a quiet child to begin with but now she was withdrawn to the point where Nikki worried. She had grown thinner, her pinched little face pale and haunted, with her two huge hazel eyes a mirror of misery. The child had one cold after another, but the only time Nikki saw her was during routine school check-ups. The teacher had drawn Nikki aside and confided her worries.

'She's often bruised,' the young teacher had whispered. 'And she "forgets" her lunch most days. I'm sure she's not getting enough to eat.'

Nikki had gone over the little girl thoroughly. There were bruises over the child's body—enough to make her approach Mrs Mears.

'She's just clumsy,' Sandra Mears had said defensively. 'She's always knocking into things.'

Nikki had watched the young woman's hands tremble as she talked. Sandra Mears was younger than Nikki—much younger. To have to cope with the burden she was facing. . .

'Sandra, can I organise you some help?' Nikki had said gently. 'I can get council child care one day a week—some time to give you a break. The four children must make you tired.'

'There's nothing wrong with me,' Sandra had snapped. 'I don't want your charity.'

'Sandra, it's not charity——'

'Well, I don't want it,' the girl had repeated, rising. 'Now butt out of what's not your business.'

'Karen's health is my business.'

'There's nothing wrong with Karen and if she says there is then she's a liar.' The girl had thinned her lips in a gesture of defiance, but still the lips had trembled.

'Now let me get Karen and I'll go home.'

And Nikki had been able to go no further. She'd talked to Karen's teacher again and then, reluctantly, had contacted the state's children's protection services. The social worker had travelled from Cairns but, like Nikki, she had hit a blank wall.

'There's not a lot I can do,' she'd told Nikki unhappily. 'I'm sure Karen's taking the brunt of her mother's unhappiness. Sandra seems deeply depressed, but neither will admit there's a problem.'

At what point should the authorities step in and remove children from a parent's care? Nikki didn't know. Unhappily she stared now at the telephone and accepted that the point might be now.

It took all her self-control not to go back to the hospital. 'I don't need you,' Luke Marriott had said. If he could get Sandra to agree to the little girl's going to hospital. . .

Well, he had as much chance as she did, if not better, Nikki thought bitterly. An autocratic male might succeed where she had failed so dismally. Maybe even egocentric surgeons had their uses! With this cheerless thought she buried her head again in her books, the hated contact lenses in place. If only she could concentrate!

Somehow Nikki managed to do some useful study. She left her books when Beattie called her for dinner, once more uneasily conscious of her new appearance. Her dress felt odd around her bare legs—like a forgotten memory. She wished she could go back to work. A white coat now would be comforting.

Luke Marriott was in the kitchen with Amy and Beattie. Amy was involved in helping Beattie serve, and Luke seemed to be supervising. In his hand he held a glass of wine, and as Nikki walked in he raised it in salutation.

'The worker emerges,' he said drily, and Nikki flushed.

'I would have described you all as the workers.'
She frowned at the glass. 'Did you buy wine,
Beattie?'

'I bought wine,' Luke told her. He filled another
glass. 'Have some.'

'No, thanks. I never do when I'm working.' She was
being a wet blanket but the man unnerved her.

'One glass isn't going to interfere——'

'I don't want it!' Nikki bit her lip, ashamed of her
outburst. 'I'm sorry,' she managed. She turned to the
housekeeper who was regarding her in astonishment.
'Can I help, Beattie?'

'I've all the help I need in young Amy here,' Beattie
told her. 'You two go in. Shoo.'

'I'll wait and help carry in the plates.' The last thing
Nikki wanted was to be alone in the dining-room with
Luke Marriott. Alone anywhere. . .

Nikki ate in silence while Beattie, Amy and Luke
chatted amiably over the events of the day. Nikki
couldn't join in. Her overwhelming emotion was anger
with herself.

Why on earth had she behaved like a tiresome child?
Nikki hadn't the faintest idea why this man was making
her react like this, and she hadn't a clue what to do
about it. Her normal, cloistered existence was shattered. She was having to share her home with a man
who made her feel. . .who made her feel like a gauche
schoolgirl.

Luke lapsed into silence as Beattie left to clear the
table, Amy virtuously helping, but he didn't seem
in the least uncomfortable. On the contrary, his
deep blue eyes held the trace of a twinkle, as if
he was aware of and enjoying the discomfiture his
presence engendered in the girl at the other end of
the table.

Finally the interminable meal came to an end and
Nikki rose. She hadn't tasted a thing and Beattie had
gone to extraordinary trouble. It was a shame.

'I'm going to put Amy to bed,' she said stiffly.

'You mean you do occasionally spend some time mothering?'

Nikki bit her lip. 'I spend heaps of time with Amy,' she said hotly. 'And Amy understands how important my job is.'

'Does she?'

'Look, I don't have to answer to you. . .'

'No,' he said slowly. 'Only to Amy.'

Nikki pushed back her chair, scraping it harshly on the polished boards. 'Amy has to understand that life is serious,' she told him. 'And work's important. Now, if you'll excuse me. . .'

'Don't you want to know about Karen?' Luke enquired, raising his brows. 'I thought a bit of professional concern might be in order.'

Nikki flushed bright red and sank down. She was going crazy. Not to have enquired. . .

'Tell me about her,' she said stiffly. 'Of course I'm worried.'

'Are you?'

'Of course I am.' Nikki bit her lip as again her anger threatened to burst out.

'So why haven't you interfered before now? You do know the child is being abused?'

'Abused. . .?'

'There are bruises all over her. And the X-ray shows the arm has been broken before.'

'Not that I'm aware of.'

'Well, it was.' Luke grimaced. 'The fracture is further up the arm from the original break. The bone's calcified around the old fracture. It happened around a year ago, I'd say.'

Nikki closed her eyes. 'I didn't. . . Neither her teacher nor I picked that up,' she whispered. 'It must have happened during the long vacation. I've seen the bruising, though.'

'And turned the other cheek?'

'I contacted community services. They sent a social worker up from Cairns.'

'That did a lot of good, I'll bet.'

Nikki rose. 'So what would you have them do?' she snapped. 'Take the children away? Sandra had Karen when she was fourteen. Fourteen! She's only twenty-two now and she has four children. She married a no-hoper, had one child after another and now he's left her and she has nothing. The community here labelled her eight years ago when she had Karen out of wedlock, and she's been isolated ever since. She struggles on to hold them together——'

'Well, she's not struggling enough,' Luke said grimly. 'I'd say she has a temper and Karen's taking the brunt of it.'

'So we take all the children?' Nikki shook her head. 'Where does that leave them—or Sandra? I asked Karen about the bruises. She told me she kept falling over—Sandra's obviously warned her about telling the truth—but if you gave her the choice of going to a strange foster home or staying with her brothers and sister, then I know the choice Karen would make.'

'So you're proposing we patch her up and send her back to face her mother's temper again.'

'No, of course not.' Nikki subsided again into her chair. Some things were just so hard. 'Not if it's reached the stage of bones being broken. But I don't know. . . I'll have to contact Cairns again.'

'The social worker?'

'Well, what else do you suggest?' Nikki demanded.

He smiled then, the blue eyes challenging. Rising, he came around to her end of the table and placed a hand on the back of her chair.

'I suggest you abandon your studies for a couple of hours,' he said firmly. 'Let's go and see Sandra now.'

'What, now?'

'As soon as Amy's in bed.' He looked at his watch. 'She won't be expecting us. It will give us a chance to assess what things are like at home, and we just might be able to do something constructive.'

'Like bring all the children back here?' Nikki said bitterly, and Luke's smile deepened. He looked around appraisingly, through the French windows to the swimming-pool beyond.

'Well, there's certainly enough room.'

'In case you hadn't noticed,' Nikki said icily, 'this is my home. And I like my privacy!'

'And I wonder why?' Luke said thoughtfully. 'This place is enormous. It needs half a dozen kids to bring it to life.'

'So you propose going and taking Sandra's? Just to keep Amy company, I suppose.'

'Dr Russell?'

Nikki looked up at him suspiciously. 'Yes?'

'Don't be so bloody stupid.'

They stopped at the hospital first. The children's ward was in darkness. The nurse rose to greet them, her finger raised to her lips in a gesture of silence.

'Karen's only just gone to sleep,' she whispered. 'Despite the medication.'

Luke frowned. 'Why? She should have drowsed off hours ago.'

'She was too frightened to go to sleep. She said. . .' The nurse hesitated. 'She kept saying we'd take her away while she was asleep.' She sighed. 'And her mother didn't come.'

'Was Karen asking for her?'

'No. But her eyes never left the door, waiting. Poor wee mite. . .'

Luke crossed silently to the bed and Nikki followed. The child was sleeping soundly in a drug-induced sleep. Her injured arm was flung out at a rigid angle. In the dim ward light her face was a wan pool of dejection. There were shadows under the huge eyes—shadows that spoke of abject misery. Nikki felt her heart wrench within her. Maybe this little one could come back to Whispering Palms for a while. . .

'Professional detachment,' Luke said softly from the other side of the bed, and Nikki raised her eyes as she realised he was watching her. 'It's a bit hard, isn't it?'

'It's impossible,' Nikki said wearily, and turned to go.

Nikki directed Luke mechanically, out past the town boundaries, along the coast road and then inland to an old farmhouse set well back from the road. This had once been the homestead for the sugar plantation it was on, but the owners had long ago wearied of the fight with white ants and age, and had rebuilt a mile further down the road. They were renting this house out for a pittance, waiting for nature to take its course.

It would soon happen. This land was natural rain-forest, and without constant clearing the forest was reclaiming its own. Huge palms surrounded the house, so much so that it was difficult to see where house started and garden ended. The veranda was sagging wearily on rotten footings, and vines and the beginnings of coconut palms were shoving up through the boards.

What a place to bring up children! The place must be crawling with snakes, Nikki thought grimly, and it was miles from anywhere. Sandra had been isolated from the Eurong community since she'd had her first child, but by living here her isolation was complete.

There was complete silence as they approached the house. A rusted-out Ford sedan stood forlornly in front of the veranda, and a light showed through a single window. They could see a vague shape through the cracked glass. The figure rose while they watched and came towards the door.

'What a dump!' Luke stood at the edge of the veranda and looked up, whistling soundlessly between his teeth. 'Surely there must be better places. . .'

'What do you want?'

Sandra was standing at the door, the solitary light behind her casting her shadow twenty feet out into the night. She was wearing a worn dressing-robe, and her long hair was matted and wild. Her figure was so thin that she appeared almost emaciated. She stood, barefoot, her arms folded. Her stance spoke of defiance and a fear so tangible that Nikki felt she could almost touch it.

'You didn't come to see Karen,' Nikki said gently. 'We thought you might.'

'Karen shouldn't be in hospital. She's only got a broken arm——'

'We're not keeping Karen in hospital because she has a broken arm,' Luke said harshly. 'Mrs Mears, may we come in?'

'No.'

Luke nodded. 'Then we'll keep Karen until the social workers arrive from Cairns,' he said firmly. 'We have no choice.'

'But——'

Luke looked up at the woman on the veranda, and in the dim light his eyes were suddenly implacable and hard. 'Mrs Mears, Karen has bruises all over her. She has a broken arm and it's not the first time it's been broken. She flinches when I raise my hand as if she's used to being beaten. And she's malnourished. Hungry, Mrs Mears. Now, are we going to come inside and talk about it, or do we contact the authorities in Cairns?'

Sandra Mears gave an audible gasp and her hand flew to her mouth. She took a step back as if Luke had slapped her.

'We need to talk, Mrs Mears.' Luke's voice had softened but was no less implacable.

There was a long silence. Then Sandra slowly turned as if sleep-walking, and walked inside.

Nikki had expected chaos. Judging from the outside, the house was a ruin and Sandra incompetent. To her amazement the place was almost pathetically clean, the cleanliness accentuating the abject poverty in the place. She looked around in amazement and then down to Sandra. Sandra had sunk to sit at the kitchen table. Her head fell forward on to her arms and her shoulders heaved. This girl was wretched, and despite her anger Nikki felt a wave of compassion. What sort of mess was this girl in?

'So tell us, what happened?'

The compassion hadn't touched Luke. He was standing over Sandra almost like the interrogator in a bad movie. Nikki put up a hand in protest but he silenced her with a look.

Sandra looked up, her tear-stained face a plea, but Luke wasn't interested in pleas. 'Tell us, Sandra,' he said.

'She. . .she broke her arm.'

'No. Tell us.'

The silence stretched out. Outside on the veranda a cane toad started its harsh croaking. The naked light-globe made the effect surrealistic and awful.

'You know,' Sandra said at last.

'No. You tell us.'

Sandra cast a scared look up at him and dashed a hand across her cheek. Luke didn't stir. His gaze didn't waver.

'She was. . .she wouldn't. . .she wouldn't do what I told her. . .' She took a deep breath. 'It's not true,' she said suddenly. 'It was Jamie. My. . .my youngest. He's four. I'd just been to town and bought some biscuits. We hadn't had biscuits for so long but. . .but the kids asked and asked. One packet of biscuits.' She looked up, pleading with them to understand. 'I just couldn't bear not to—so I got them and then I went outside and when I come back Jamie had got at them and eaten six and shoved the rest in the toilet 'cos he was full and he didn't know what to do with the half-eaten packet and was scared I'd find them. And they

blocked the toilet and I found them and I hit Jamie,
but I couldn't hit him hard 'cos he's only four and he
gets asthma, and then Karen started crying and said I
shouldn't hit him and. . .and I just——' Her voice
broke off into tears.

'So you hit Karen instead,' Luke said, and to Nikki's
surprise his voice had gentled.

'Yeah.' The girl's face came up. 'I always do. She's
so like me. She just stands there and takes it. She
doesn't even cry. She just stands there. The other kids
were crying 'cos they hadn't had any biscuits but not
Karen. . .'

'She's so like you. . .'

'Yeah.' Sandra's head sank on to her arms and she
gave a broken sob. 'I feel so bad. I love her so much
and I hurt her. . .' She managed to look up again.
'Maybe it's best if you take her away. I know I'll keep
hurting her. And I love her.' She gave a desperate
gulp as if to gain strength to continue. 'I know it sounds
crazy but I love her more than the rest of the kids put
together and yet I hurt her. . .'

'You didn't come to the hospital. . .'

'She'd look at me,' Sandra said brokenly. 'I know
she'd just look at me and not say anything. She won't
even cry.'

Luke sat down at the bare, scrubbed table and his
hand came out to cover Sandra's. 'Mrs Mears, you've
reached the point where you accept help or watch your
family disintegrate,' he said softly. He motioned backwards to where Nikki was standing, silently watching.
'Dr Russell and I can help, but only if you let us.
You've admitted there's a problem. If you love your
daughter, then you must admit that you need help.
And then accept it.'

Sandra's eyes once more met his. There was a long
silence. Even the cane toad outside had hushed. Nikki
found she was holding her breath. So much depended
on these next few moments.

Then Sandra took a ragged breath, and then another. She looked over to Nikki and back to Luke.

'I'm in trouble,' she whispered. 'I don't know what to do. Please. . .please help me.'

Luke nodded as if he had expected no less. His hand stayed exactly where it was, and Nikki had a sudden sense of how Sandra must feel. To have this man touching her, feeding strength, reassurance and warmth into her through his touch. There was a sudden, crazy moment of irrational jealousy, quickly stifled.

Luke stood, and motioned to Nikki. 'Do we have any sleeping-pills, Dr Russell?'

'Yes.' Nikki frowned. She wouldn't have thought leaving sleeping-tablets for this woman was the most sensible thing. Sandra seemed almost suicidal.

'We'll leave you two tablets for the night,' Luke told Sandra, heading off Nikki's criticism. 'I want you to take them and get a solid night's sleep. Tomorrow morning I want you to get up, wash your hair, put on your nicest dress and bring the children into the hospital. I'll arrange the nursing staff to take care of them for the rest of the day. You'll visit Karen and then meet me in my surgery at twelve.'

'My surgery'. Nikki flinched on the words. This man had taken right over. Still, he had achieved more so far than she had ever been able to with this sullen, frightened girl.

'But——'

'No buts.' Luke was standing, still not taking his eyes from Sandra. 'By twelve tomorrow I'll have a list of options available for you, and I want you to come knowing that every option is better than what's happening now.'

'But there's nothing. . .' It was a frightened whisper.

'There's everything.' Once more, Luke's voice gentled and his hand came down on to her shoulder. 'There's a whole great world out here for you and your children, Sandra, and it's time you started finding it.'

'But Karen. . .'

'Karen loves you.' He smiled then and his smile warmed the bleak little room. 'If I didn't think that, I wouldn't help you. But Karen loves you and she's a smart little girl. She wouldn't love you unless you were worth loving. So let's get to work and repay her trust.'

They left her then, sitting staring out bleakly into the night. Nikki was aware of intense disquiet as they bumped down the overgrown track away from the house.

'You don't think she'll do anything stupid, do you?' she said softly.

Luke flashed her a quizzical look. 'Like suicide?'

'Like suicide.'

He shook his head. 'She loves her family too much.'

'You sounded tougher before you met her.'

Luke nodded as he manoeuvred the little car out on to the road and turned homewards. 'She's OK.' He was talking almost to himself. 'Sometimes life is just too much. I think for Sandra it's reached that point. But now she's said she needs help—well, I reckon there's light at the end of her tunnel, anyway.'

Nikki frowned across at him. His voice had suddenly flattened as if he was doing some sort of personal comparison. Surely this self-confident, overbearing male couldn't have major problems in his life. And yet. . . He was at Eurong for a reason. What on earth was it?

'Tell me why you're doing country locums,' she said gently, and he flashed her a look of amusement.

'Probing into my ghosts, Dr Russell?'

Nikki flushed. 'You're a successful surgeon,' she continued, and was annoyed at the trace of resentment she heard in her voice. 'Why. . .why have you given it up?'

'I haven't given it up.'

'Doing a locum in a backwater like Eurong is hardly a strategic career move,' she said waspishly.

'No.' He smiled across at her. 'Neither is burying yourself here in a house too big for you in a community that's known and labelled you from childhood. And that's what you're doing, Dr Russell.'

Nikki bit her lip angrily. 'Beattie——' she started.

'If you think I can practise for half a day in this place and not learn all the local gossip, you don't know much about the town you live in,' he told her.

'Especially when you ask!'

He grinned. 'Especially when I ask.'

The car slowed suddenly and Nikki looked out. They were still two miles from home on the beach road. Luke was pulling the little car on to the kerb, and coming to a halt.

'Wh-what are you doing?' Nikki stammered.

'I've been in a stuffy surgery all day,' Luke told her. 'And the moon is full and the beach is calling. I'm taking a short walk, Dr Russell. Are you coming or do you intend to sit in the car and sulk while I walk?'

'But. . .'

Luke didn't hear. The car was stationary and Luke had left, striding swiftly around to hold the door open for her. 'Coming, Dr Russell?'

A walk on the beach was how Nikki often ended her day. After hours spent trying to solve everyone else's problems, the sea and the moonlight were often the only way she could calm her tired mind. But to walk with this man. . .

She looked up, and his eyes held a challenge. Afraid? they mocked, and suddenly she knew she was. She didn't want this. She didn't want what seemed to be happening whether she wanted it or not.

'Don't be so bloody stupid,' he said, for the second time that night, and his eyes mocked her.

Nikki took a deep breath. 'I should be in bed,' she said tightly.

He held up the car keys. 'Well, the car's going nowhere,' he said gently. He held out his hand to take hers. Helplessly Nikki felt herself drawn up and out of the car. 'A walk,' he said firmly. 'Nothing else, Dr Russell. Not yet.'

CHAPTER FOUR

THE night was still and warm. A gentle breeze from the sea stopped it being oppressively hot. October on the coast along the Great Barrier Reef was the loveliest of months—the time before the real oppression of the steamy wet season began.

Nikki walked slowly down towards the sea. As she had risen from the car Luke had released her hand and had gone before, leaving her to follow if she would. Now he strode easily across the firm, tide-washed sand, his face lifting to the moonlight as though soaking in its beauty.

Once more Nikki found herself wondering about this man of many parts. How many men took time to soak up the loveliness of a night like this?

What had she expected? That he would use this opportunity to make a pass at her? He seemed now to be oblivious to her presence, and Nikki knew that Luke would have stopped the car and walked even if he'd been alone.

As he was now. He walked alone across the moonlit beach, alone with whatever demons drove him, and Nikki was left to her own demons.

And they were there. The ghosts from Nikki's past were never far from this place. Her parents. Scott. . .

What was Scott doing now? Married again? Of course he'd be married, Nikki told herself bitterly. Scott was charming and personable and desperate for money. He'd be married now to some lady who could support the lifestyle he craved.

Bitterness at the past rose up in her, threatening to overwhelm her. How could he have treated her like that? Men were bastards, she thought bleakly, remembering Sandra Mears' haggard face. She and Sandra both. . .

Why on earth hadn't she been able to see Scott's true colours before she'd been crazy enough to marry him? She'd been so stupid.

Well, it wasn't going to happen again. Not ever. She needed no one and Amy was solely dependent on her. Amy would be brought up with security and love, but no man was needed.

The bitter words Scott had flung at her had stayed in her heart for five long years. He had called her a lying, deceitful whore. He had laughed at her for believing that he had married her for love—he'd told her that no one would ever want her for herself alone.

Nikki took a deep breath and turned her face into the warm night air. The bitterness was all around her, and she was so alone. She looked down to the water's edge at Luke, and a sense of empathy edged into her consciousness. Somehow this man was alone as she.

It was curiously comforting. The soft night wind whipped the fine fabric of her dress around her bare legs. Her hair blew lightly around her face and she drank in the salt air greedily.

Something was happening to her. She didn't know what it was but she only knew that something inside her was being released—just a little—from the bondage that Scott had imposed. Was it Charlotte's crazy, impulsive action in forcing her into attractive clothes? Or was it something else?

Luke was walking slowly back up the beach towards her, his face in shadow with the moon behind him. As he reached her he held out his hands and Nikki took an involuntary step back.

'I'm not going to rape you,' he said easily, and there was a trace of mocking laughter in his voice. 'Oh, so scared, Miss Prim. Why?'

'I'm not scared.' Nikki sounded like a defiant child.

He nodded as though humouring her, then sank on

to the sand and hauled his shoes off. Then his socks.
Then. . .

'What are you doing?' Nikki gaped open-mouthed,
and then blushed crimson as she realised just what he
intended.

'I'm going for a swim, of course.' She couldn't see
his face but there was no mistaking the laughter.
'Coming?'

This was something Nikki had done in the long-
forgotten past. Eurong beach stretched for miles and
the tiny population meant that it was almost always
deserted. Eurong was not a tourist destination—the
locals kept its beauty as a closely guarded secret—and
it meant it was possible to come down here, strip to
nothing and swim undisturbed.

The last time Nikki had done such a thing had been
five years ago—five years. . .

'Don't be. . .' Nikki turned away with a gasp as she
realised her protest was falling on deaf ears. His naked
body in the moonlight was breathtaking—and the last
thing she wanted to do was look. 'I'll. . .I'll wait for
you in the car.'

'It's a magnificent night,' he protested, still half
laughing. 'Why waste it on prudery, Miss Prim?'

'I'm not. . .'

'You don't have to strip,' he told her. 'Or are you
worried about spoiling your beautiful new clothes?'

'I'm. . .'

'Scared?' To Nikki's horror she felt his hands grip
her shoulders. His body touched the soft fabric of her
dress, sending a sensuous shiver through her skin.
'Life's short,' he said softly. 'And you're wasting it,
Dr Russell. You wouldn't really go back to bury yourself in books tonight, would you?'

'Let me go.' Nikki wrenched herself away but was
no match for his strength.

'Why?' His voice softened and the humour faded.
'Nikki, life is for living. God knows what tomorrow

holds. Surely you can't ignore tonight?' His grip on her shoulders tightened. 'Look up. The stars are magnificent. The sea is ours. The night is ours, Dr Russell, and I don't intend to go tamely home to bed. And I can't soak it up if I know you're sitting in the car tapping your fingers on the dashboard with impatience. So, as far as I see it, there's only one thing for it.'

'I——'

'You're going to have to come in too.'

'No!' Nikki's cry of refusal was cut off in a staccato shriek. It was ignored. In one fluid movement Luke Marriott had dropped his hands to her waist and pulled her up into his arms.

There was nothing she could do. Nikki was cradled helplessly against him, powerless to struggle. Heedless of the futility of her actions, she crashed her fists into his bare chest. It was as much use as a moth fluttering against a lighted window. Luke's chest showed as little impact, and he strode purposefully forward.

'Put me down.' It was a cry of outrage. No man had touched Nikki Russell for five years and she had no intention of permitting it now. Especially not this man!

'I'll put you down,' Luke promised drily, 'when I'm ready.'

'But——'

'Dr Russell, you are withering into dust with your old house and your elderly housekeeper and your books. Beattie has more life in her than you and she's near seventy. Your housekeeper says you need something to cheer you up, and I've taken it on board as a personal challenge.'

'If you think dumping me in the water will cheer me up. . .!' She pummelled again and her feet lashed out, but he kept right on walking, implacably quiet, towards the water.

And Nikki fell silent, speechless. The feel of Luke's hard body under her was doing crazy, crazy things to her equilibrium. This was mad. Her whole world was mad.

'I'm not dumping you in the water,' he said cheerfully as they neared the shallows. 'I'm taking you for a swim.'

'There are stingers in the water. And stingrays.'

'Beattie tells me the stingers won't be here for another few weeks,' he reassured her kindly. 'And with the amount of noise you've been making, any self-respecting stingray will have lit out for Texas ten minutes ago. Now shut up, hold your nose and enjoy yourself.'

'But. . .'

She got no further. While Luke had been talking he had broached the waves at the water's edge. Now they were surging around his waist, and as Nikki uttered her last word a large crest surged towards them, shoulder-high. Luke simply lifted his burden and deposited her neatly into the foaming surf.

Nikki had forgotten what it would be like. . . She had expected coldness—shock—but. . .the tropical water was almost warm. It had been five long years since Nikki had granted herself the indulgence of a beach swim and, despite her shock and anger, her overwhelming sensation was that of being welcomed back by a friend. She had loved the sea. Now it folded her back into its clasp with a sensual pleasure that was almost a caress.

Involuntarily Nikki felt her body moving into a graceful dive, turning away from the man throwing her into the wave and sweeping under the crest in a lithe arcing of her slim body.

Oh, it was lovely! Why had she stayed away for so long? The salt water surrounded her, encasing her in its cool caress, cooling her overheated body, taking the shards from her anger. . .

What on earth was she doing? She wasn't swimming! There were texts she hadn't opened yet and she was in the water, cavorting. . .

She rose unsteadily to her feet, her feet finding the sandy bottom. Her dress clung and swayed around her legs, pulled by the strength of the water. Luke was only feet from her, his eyes in the dim moonlight amused and appreciative.

'Well, well,' he said slowly. 'The lady can swim. Now, why does Beattie tell me you haven't swum in the sea for years?'

'It's none of your business,' Nikki spluttered, trying to stalk forward. Another wave pounded into her back, making her stumble and spoiling the effect of her damping words entirely. Where on earth was her dignity? Before she could fall, strong arms reached out and held her.

'It's OK to have fun,' Luke Marriott said softly, looking down at the sodden girl in his arms. 'It's OK, Nikki.'

'Well, this is hardly my idea of fun,' Nikki snapped. 'To be half drowned. . .'

'You? Half drowned? You can swim like a fish.'

'You didn't know that when you threw me under!'

'No.' He was staring down at her in the soft light. 'I didn't. But I could guess. As I can guess a hell of a lot about you, Nikki Russell.'

'Well, keep your guesswork for someone else.' Nikki was almost crying. 'I don't want it. I don't want you anywhere near me.'

'Or anyone else,' he said softly. 'At least, that's what you say.'

'It's true.'

'No.' He shook his head. 'You have needs, just like the rest of us, Dr Russell.'

'I don't. . .'

'Well, let's just see.' His grip suddenly tightened. Her body was drawn hard against his naked chest and his blond head sank to kiss her.

Nikki froze. His lips took hers to him, yet they couldn't force her to respond. Her mouth was hard, immobile, and then her hands came up to shove him away.

It was that movement that was her undoing. Her fingers touched his wet, bare skin and a tremor ran through her. Five years. Five long years of nothing. . .

And now this. Lips that searched hers, hands that held her hard against him, making her body feel his strength—his maleness. Her dress might not have existed. Wet and limp, it was a frail barrier between them, and Nikki's body knew his beneath it.

His hands held her tighter, tighter still, pulling her to compliance, moulding her breasts into his muscled chest. Waves of salt foam swept in and out around them but the surging water just deepened the caress, isolating them more against the world.

And to her horror Nikki felt herself respond. The night was magic. This moment was magic. The warmth of the water, the light of the waning moon and the sweeping whisper of the surf all combined to drug her into euphoria. She was powerless to resist. Powerless. . .

Slowly, slowly, her lips parted, allowing his insistent tongue to enter. He tasted of the sea, salt and something else. . .something of the night and the mood and the maleness of him.

Oh, God, she was mad and yet she couldn't stop. It was as if she were indeed drowning and this man's body was the only thing between her and the end of the world. There was the ocean around them. They were an island in the sea and they were stranded forever. His hands fell to her hips, caressing her thighs, pulling her in to feel his maleness, and she felt her body mould to him. If she were to die now, this was what heaven would feel like. She arched back, her neck white and satin-sheened in the moonlight, and from a distance she heard herself moan. The sound held pain and desire and. . .

And what? Who could know?

His mouth fell to the swell of her breasts, and the top button of her dress was suddenly undone. A hand went in to tease the tautness of her nipples and Nikki moaned again.

And then the sea intervened. A surge of surf, larger than the rest, tossed itself at the entwined couple. They staggered together and Luke's hand fell away to save them both from falling.

It was enough. The tiny movement of withdrawal was enough to give Nikki back her senses. With a gasp of horror she pulled away, her hands coming up to cover the gaping nakedness of her breasts. Mad. She was mad. They were both mad.

And then they were staring at each other over the moon-drenched sea and Luke's eyes reflected what Nikki was feeling. There was horror in his eyes as well, and Nikki knew that he too had not intended what had just happened.

'Nikki. . .' Luke's voice was unsteady, uncertain, for the first time since Nikki had met him. Nikki shook her head and turned away.

'I'll be in the car,' she whispered. 'When you're ready. . .'

Luke dressed swiftly on the beach while Nikki sat sodden in the car, waiting. When he came, she was hunched as far away as it was possible to be on the passenger side of the car and, after one swift, hard glance at his companion, Luke started the car and turned for home. They drove home in silence.

Luke's face was set and grim, and his customary cheerfulness seemed to have deserted him. It was almost as though he was as shaken as she was, Nikki thought bitterly, though such a thing was hardly possible. A 'love 'em and leave 'em' man, was Luke Marriott, if Charlotte's information could be relied on.

Which it could be, Nikki thought. To do this. . .to seduce her. . .

He hadn't seduced her. He had kissed her and she had responded. That truth made Nikki hug her arms into her breasts and shiver, and Luke cast a glance across at her.

'My sweater's over the back,' he said impersonally, and another shudder ran through Nikki's body. How could he? How could he act as if nothing had happened?

Maybe it was the only way to act, but some emotion which Nikki could not define was running between them, and to talk—to try for impersonal conversation —would somehow strengthen that emotion. The tension scared Nikki half to death and, by the look of it, Luke also didn't know how to react.

Good, she thought nastily. To get the great Luke Marriott off balance. . .

Curiously the thought didn't help at all. All it did was make her want to cry.

Finally the little car pulled off the road into the driveway of Whispering Palms. Nikki looked out in relief at the sight of her home—her refuge. If only she could turn to Luke Marriott and tell him it was no longer his. That he should find somewhere else—even if it did mean sleeping on a park bench!

She turned to him and found him watching her, but before she could speak he laid a finger on her lips.

'I'm sorry, Nikki,' he said gently. 'I should never have kissed you.'

The great Luke Marriott apologising! Nikki could hardly believe her ears, and yet all it did was make her urge to burst into tears even greater. And then, before she could respond, before she could realise what he intended, his head came down and his lips touched hers.

It was a kiss of contrition—a feather-light kiss that

should have caused no feeling. She had been kissed many times like that before. Instead Nikki felt her heart turn within her. She put a hand up to touch his face but he had already withdrawn.

'And I'm sorry for that, too,' he said unsteadily. 'It won't happen again.'

How was a girl supposed to study after that?

Heaven knew. Nikki didn't. She showered the salt and sand from her body, donned a housecoat, rinsed her sodden dress and then went to tackle her texts. It was the last thing she wanted to do, but she had wasted so much time!

What was Luke doing? The words of the text danced before her eyes in a meaningless jumble. What on earth was she trying to study?

Hearing difficulties. . .problems with the ear. . . She had to concentrate. If she kept going like this, she'd fail.

And then what? A thin, insistent little voice started up in the back of her head. So what if you fail? There's always next year. And your income doesn't depend on it.

What on earth was she saying? This was work she was rejecting, and one thing Nikki Russell hadn't done in the last five years was reject work. It was only a matter of blocking out the thought of Luke Marriott. The memory of his hands. . .his lips. . .

Damn the man. She stared down at her page and started to read aloud, forcing her tired mind back on to track. 'Tinnitus. . .ringing in the ears. . .' What on earth did she know about tinnitus?

'Do you need some help?'

Nikki jumped close to a foot in the air. The house had been deathly still and she hadn't heard Luke come up behind her. Now she nearly dropped her text as he placed his hands on the back of her chair and read over her shoulder. 'You shouldn't be working,' he said conversationally. 'But if you insist, then I'll give you a hand.'

'Thanks, but I don't need it.' It was as much as Nikki could do to get the words out.

'What do you need, then?' he quizzed her gently. 'You tell me you don't need a walk. You don't need a swim. You don't need help.' He smiled down at her, his mobile eyebrows arched upwards. 'I'm a paid employee, Dr Russell. So start employing me.'

Nikki shoved her book down on the desk with a bang and rose unsteadily to her feet. She should be wearing something more substantial than her flimsy housecoat. It was sheer cotton and not respectable in the least.

'I'm employing you to attend to my normal medical duties,' she said tightly. 'And I'm. . . I don't want anything else.'

He wasn't listening. Luke had picked up the text she had just dropped. 'OK,' he said absently. 'What are the three types of tinnitus?'

'Look——'

'What are they, Dr Russell?'

Nikki stared helplessly at him. Arguing was impossible. The man was like a bulldozer. She forced herself to focus on what he was saying.

Tinnitus. Types. What were they?

'Low-frequency noise, like hearing the sea,' she started hesitantly.

'Cause?'

'Typically impacted wax. Or maybe otosclerosis.'

'Good,' he approved. 'Next type?'

'High-frequency noise, like a cicada,' Nikki told him. Her hand was on the back of her chair as if for support, but her mind was steadying as she focused on work. 'Suggestive of inner ear pathology such as ototoxicity, trauma or tumour compressing the nerve.'

'And the last?'

'Look, you don't have to do this.'

'I wasted your time taking you swimming. Now I'm making amends. Next, Dr Russell.'

'I don't——'

'Think, Dr Russell.' Luke's voice was clipped and professional, reminding Nikki of nothing so much as her old professors, grilling her until she was exhausted during final exams. She took a deep breath. She knew. She had to know.

And it was there, locked in the recess of her tired mind. She brought it out and dusted it off. 'Pulsatile tinnitus,' she said hesitantly. 'Noise coinciding with the patient's heart-rate.'

'That's the onè. And cause?'

'I don't know.' Then at his look of disgust she changed her mind. 'Yes, I do. Intercranial vascular lesion, for instance jugular tumour.'

'And if you can't treat tinnitus, what do you do about it?' Luke demanded, and Nikki stared.

'I thought you were a surgeon,' she muttered. 'Surgeons never admit you can't treat something.'

He smiled then, his eyes weary but acknowledging a hit. 'This is an exam for general practitioners,' he smiled, 'not for surgeons. Let's assume we've done our worst—all the medical possibilities are exhausted, the surgeons have sent your patient back to you with a "too hard" label on him and your patient still has ringing in his ears. What then, Dr Russell?'

'Antidepressant?'

'It can make the noise more tolerable,' Luke agreed. 'But then what? Do you leave your patient taking pills for the rest of his or her life? The examiners won't like your answer, Dr Russell.'

Nikki flushed. 'Well, the accepted treatment is the use of white noise,' she said stiffly. 'A noise simulator which produces something like the noise of a running stream, or rain on a tin roof. Most unmedical, but effective.'

'And that's what this exam is all about,' Luke told

her. 'How Nikki Russell has learned to dispense medicine in the real world, and knows when to shove the prescription pad aside.'

'It sounds as if you know it all,' Nikki said resentfully.

'And I'm just a surgeon.' He flipped to the next page. 'What next?'

Nikki moved to the door. 'I'm going to bed.'

He shook his head. 'You intended to work for at least a couple of hours before I appeared, didn't you, Dr Russell?'

Nikki nodded reluctantly. 'But I can't now.'

'Yes, you can.' He moved back to block her exit from the door. 'Dr Russell, I am here to ensure you pass this exam, come hell or high water. And it's only come Dr Marriott. So sit down and answer questions. Now, Dr Russell!'

'But——'

'Sit down,' he said quietly, but his low voice held the trace of a threat. 'Sit or I'll sit you down in a way you'll find distinctly undignified.'

Nikki stared up at his face, but the humour was gone. His eyes were stern and implacable.

And she did want to pass this exam. If he could really help. . .

She sat.

To Nikki's amazement the ensuing two hours were the most productive she had spent so far. What had passed between them earlier in the night had somehow been driven aside. It was still there, latent, unresolved, but it was another part of them. The professional part— the part that had put them through stringent medical training—was in play and it produced the most effective study Nikki had done. When the big grandfather clock in the hall struck midnight she lifted her head in amazement.

'Thank you,' she said simply. 'I will go to bed now.'

'To sleep?' The blue eyes watching her saw too much.

'Of course.'

'The shadows let you sleep, then?'

'What. . .? What do you mean?' Unconsciously Nikki clutched the neckline of her housecoat as though seeking warmth from its flimsy fabric. 'What do you mean—shadows?'

'They stand out a mile,' Luke told her. He stood, stretching his long limbs. He was barefoot, wearing light cotton trousers and a soft, short-sleeved shirt, open at the throat. The two of them could be taken for a married couple, Nikki thought suddenly, and then grimaced. It was a crazy scenario—the two of them alone at this hour. Beattie was long since gone to bed and the house was in whispering stillness. The palms along the veranda which gave the house its name murmured in hushed tones in the night breeze.

'You're crazy.' Nikki stood too and then wished she hadn't. The movement brought her too close to Luke. She half expected him to move back, but he stayed, looking down at her.

'Tell me about Scott,' he said softly.

CHAPTER FIVE

Scott. . .

The name flashed before them like a cruel sword, knifing at Nikki's heart.

How had Luke. . .?

'Tell me about him,' he repeated gently.

What sort of questioning was this? Nikki's eyes widened. She stared up at Luke with anger flashing, but Luke's eyes were reflective and calm.

'No,' she whispered.

Luke was between Nikki and the door. Nikki put out a hand to shove him aside but he caught and held it. Her hand lay in his, warmth against warmth, and Nikki's anger turned to an overwhelming feeling of distress. She pulled again but the grip tightened.

'Look, it's none of your business,' she managed. 'I don't know how you found out about Scott. . .'

'Beattie,' he smiled. 'How else?'

'Well, Beattie has no right to talk about me. Beattie, Charlotte, and now you!' Nikki's voice rose in anger. 'All of you think you can interfere with my life. Well, I don't want it. I don't need your interrogation. . .'

'You don't need anybody.' Luke's eyes were still calm, the deep blue penetrating into the depths of her heart. His look was like a red-hot torch, burning in. Nikki had never felt anything like it in her life before. This man could see parts of her that had remained hidden for years—that she had sworn would never again be revealed. 'You do, though, Nikki,' he said softly. 'And whatever is hurting needs to be talked of. So tell me.'

'No.'

He shook his head. 'Nikki, I'm only here for three

weeks. Then I get out of your life forever. But for those three weeks I intend getting rid of the shadows—or at least having a damned good try. You need someone to talk to. So talk to me.'

'I don't want to.' It was practically a wail, and Luke smiled.

'Yes, you do,' he told her, and pulled her firmly in to lie against him. His hand came up to run through her mass of golden-red curls and his fingers sent warmth and reassurance through her body. 'Beattie tells me you've been carrying this for five years. It's too long to carry bitterness and hate. So tell me.'

Nikki held her body stiffly, resentfully, but the fingers did their work insidiously. His hand moved against her head, sending messages of reassurance and comfort through her. Let the bitterness go, his hand was telling her. Tell me. Tell someone. Spill it out. And he wouldn't release her until she did. . .

'Scott was my husband,' she said stiffly, reluctantly. 'But I suppose Beattie told you that.'

'And he left you?'

'Yes.' It was crazy talking to this man, cradled against his shoulder like a child needing comfort. She didn't feel like a child, though. Nikki felt every inch a woman and her body was achingly aware of his.

And yet. . . And yet she could talk to him. This was a comfort she had never known—a peace she had never been blessed with.

'Scott and I grew up together,' she said slowly. She was talking into the soft folds of Luke's shirt. His face was above hers. She could feel the beating of his heart. There was no need to talk above a whisper.

'Scott's father was a fisherman,' she continued. 'But Scott hankered for life away from here. We went to university together in Brisbane—Scott to do law and me to do medicine.' She sighed. 'Scott's motives— well, I'm not sure why he wanted to do law—but my mother had severe rheumatoid arthritis and ever since

I was tiny I'd been frustrated by not being able to help. So we went to Brisbane—two kids from a tiny town—and we just kept on together. Scott was always there. Just as he'd been when I was small.'

'Your parents were wealthy?'

Nikki stiffened in Luke's hold but his fingers didn't pause in their gentle stroking. He was way ahead of her. He could read her mind, this man. It seemed that she didn't need to tell him anything. He knew.

'My father was the son of a British peer,' Nikki said bitterly. 'He had a fight with his father, came to Australia when he was a teenager, married my mother and stayed. Money was never a problem for us—or at least it never appeared a problem. Dad was Lord Peter Russell, and he never stopped using the Lord. My mother's family left us Whispering Palms but my father always implied that he was humouring her by living in her childhood home rather than something much more grand. My father didn't work. He spent heaps on my mother and me, and he made it sound as though he had lots for me to inherit. That's why. . .'

'That's why Scott asked you to marry him.'

Nikki writhed in Luke's grasp but his hold didn't ease. Instead it tightened and the waves of warmth and reassurance increased. 'Tell me, Nikki,' he said.

'Of course it was why he asked me to marry him,' Nikki said reluctantly. 'But I was too stupid to see. I didn't realise that the only reason someone so vibrant—so alive—as Scott would want to be with me was because he was on to something he couldn't get any other way.' She shook her head and angry tears started behind her eyes.

'Scott and I were married while we were still at university,' she continued bitterly. 'We were happy for a while. And then, just as I graduated, my mother died. And my father—the man who I always thought was the strong one—couldn't face what was left behind. He took what he believed was the only way out.'

Luke gave an almost soundless whistle. 'Tough!' he said softly.

'It was.' Nikki put a hand up to wipe away angry tears but Luke was before her, his hand taking the tears away from her eyes. 'But it got worse. After his funeral they gave me a note which he'd left with his lawyer.' She took a deep breath. 'My father left a note saying the money had finished a couple of years earlier—that he couldn't face life without money and he was deep in debt. He'd managed to hide it until my mother had died but now. . . Now the only way for him was suicide. . .'

'And Scott?' Luke's voice was grim.

'Scott!' Nikki laughed, a harsh, tight little sound that was caught by Luke's nearness. 'At first Scott was so supportive. He was marvellous when my mother died, and when they found my father. I remember thinking, At least I have Scott. With Scott I can face this. Only then—the night of the funeral—the lawyer gave me the note and Scott and I read it together. And then. . . and then we sat down and went through my father's desk and realised that after coping with the bills there would be nothing.'

'I see.'

Luke did see. From his voice Nikki knew she didn't have to say the rest. It came out, though. It seemed as if it had to.

'At first I thought Scott was just upset for me—but then. . .then I said that at least we still had Whispering Palms. It was my mother's. She. . .she must have known about my father's debts. The house was left in trust for our. . .for my children, so it couldn't be sold. So at least we had a home. . .'

'And Scott wasn't impressed.'

Nikki shrugged listlessly. 'Scott said he was damned if he was working hard for the rest of his life. He said he'd been conned. He said he'd been trapped into marriage—that my father had led him to believe there were millions. And that much was true,' Nikki admitted. 'My father had always talked big. And Scott. . . well, Scott just stood up at the end of it and said, "That's it, Nikki. This is where I get off." And he walked out. Just like that. Just like. . .just like my father. "This is where I get off".'

Nikki fell silent. She stood motionless against Luke while his fingers did their work. 'I never saw him again,' she whispered finally. 'He wrote once, to ask for a divorce. But that was all. . .'

'Well.' Luke's fingers had stilled but now they started again. 'That must have been some week out of your life, Nikki.'

She shrugged. 'In that week I had my pregnancy confirmed. In that week. . .well, it was the week I found out what the world is really all about.'

'What Scott was all about,' Luke said grimly. 'You can't judge the world by your father's weakness and Scott's appalling behaviour. You can't, Nikki.' He put her away from him then, his hands holding her shoulders at arm's length, allowing him to look into her tear-drenched eyes. 'Believe me, you can't.'

And for a moment she almost believed him. Nikki looked up into the depths of those eyes and found her world shifting. She could drown in those eyes. She could let herself go. She could be as big a fool over this man as she had been over Scott.

Then from nowhere Charlotte's words came crashing into her head to haul her back to reality. 'Luke Marriott had every junior nurse, some senior ones, and a few female doctors besides, making fools of themselves every time he walked past. He's broken more hearts than I care to name.' Charlotte's words echoed over and over again until Nikki came to her senses.

Luke Marriott wasn't breaking her heart. She wasn't

going to make a fool of herself. Not again. She couldn't bear it. With an angry thrust she put herself away from him and whirled to face the door.

'I know I can't keep judging,' she said bitterly, 'but I can make darned sure I'm not such a fool again.'

'If you don't trust, then you can't love,' he said softly.

She turned back to face him. 'Well, who can I trust?' she demanded. 'Are you to be trusted? I don't even know why the hell you're here, Luke Marriott. You should be sitting back in Cairns with your adoring nursing staff and your highly paid surgical career. . .'

'That's right,' he said equitably. 'I should be.'

'So why the hell aren't you?' Nikki had gone past the point of courtesy. This man had left her raw and exposed and she wanted to lash back—at any cost. 'Why aren't you there? What are you running from?'

'I'm not running from anything.'

'No?' Nikki gave a bitter laugh. 'Something had to go wrong in your life to make you give up such a lucrative profession as your surgical career. I've told you my pathetic past, Luke Marriott. Now you show me your shadows.'

Luke's eyes darkened. For a moment Nikki thought he would walk out of the room in anger, without replying. Then his look changed.

'Fair enough,' he said softly. 'You did tell me.'

'So. . .? So why did you leave Cairns in such a hurry?' The words came out slowly as Nikki's anger died. Suddenly she wasn't sure she wanted to know his reason. And when it came, she was sure of it.

'There was a very good reason,' he said slowly. 'I had cancer.'

Cancer. . .

The word echoed around and around the small room. Nikki stared across at Luke as if he had physically struck her.

'Cancer,' she said blankly.

'That's right.'

She took a deep breath. 'What. . .what sort. . .?'

'Hodgkin's disease.'

It had to be, she thought dully. Hodgkin's disease was a cancer of the lymph glands, often presenting in otherwise healthy young males. Nikki had seen a couple of cases in her practice. One had died and Nikki still cringed at the tragic waste.

'Yes.'

'I. . .I see.'

'No.' He shook his head and his eyes were suddenly far-away. 'I bet you don't see, Dr Russell. Only some-one who's faced cancer themselves can see what a diagnosis like that can do to you.'

'It must. . .it must have been frightening.'

He shrugged. 'What do you think?' He closed his eyes momentarily. 'I don't think I've ever been so scared in my whole life.'

Nikki moistened her lips, searching for the right words. In the end she found refuge in medicine—a doctor's approach.

'How did you find it?'

'I had night sweats,' he said shortly. 'I'd been work-ing too damned hard and was feeling pretty run down. Then I started waking drenched with sweat. For a while I told myself I was imagining things. Then I found a swollen lymph node in my neck.'

'Weight loss?'

'No.' He smiled without humour. 'I was living too well for that.'

Still. . . Nikki's mind was racing. Without weight loss, he'd caught it early.

'So you had tests in Cairns?'

'No.' Luke grimaced. 'I can put two and two together pretty fast, even if I was hoping to hell I was making fourteen. I was at the end of a job in Cairns. An oncologist friend, Rod Olsing, who worked with me for a while in Cairns, had just moved to Sydney, so I rang him and took myself down there.'

'Why?'

He shrugged again. His habitual smile was gone, replaced with bleak remembrance.

'Cowardice, if you like. In Cairns I'd been successful and totally in control. Suddenly I was badly out of control and I couldn't face it. So I went south and faced it there.'

'And it was bad?' Nikki's voice had softened in automatic sympathy.

'Yeah. It was bad.' He gave a short laugh. 'And there's nothing like lying in a strange hospital thinking you're facing death for making you look at life. Or what you've been calling life.'

'You had radiotherapy?'

'And chemotherapy.' Luke dug his hands deep in his pockets and turned away. 'The X-rays and CT scan were clear, thank God. The glands in the neck were the only ones affected, but the night sweats made me stage 1B instead of stage 1A. Hence they gave me the works.'

Nikki nodded. The appearance of a single tumour would usually be treated just by radiotherapy. The night sweats would mean chemotherapy, though. Involuntarily her eyes went to Luke's shock of blond hair and he caught her look as he turned back to face her.

'It's grown back nicely,' he said grimly, touching his hair. 'That's the least of the side-effects.'

Nikki nodded sympathetically. 'But you've been in remission now for. . .?'

'For close on two years.'

'But that means there's every chance you're cured. The cure-rate for Hodgkin's is. . .'

'Over seventy per cent if it's caught at stage one. I know, Dr Russell; believe me, I know.'

'Well, then.' Nikki took a deep breath. 'Well, then, why aren't you getting on with life again?'

'I am.'

'By running?'

'I'm not running.'

'So what are you doing here? Isn't your career centred on the city? You'll never get anywhere doing three-week locums.'

He shook his head. 'On the contrary, Dr Russell. I'll never get anywhere by being a successful city surgeon.' He touched her hair lightly with his finger. 'And now, if you'll excuse me, Dr Russell, your locum is going to bed.'

To bed but not to sleep.

Nikki lay for hours watching the light of the full moon gradually move across her ceiling. The big ceiling fan whirred lazily, mesmerically, over her head. Usually it soothed her to sleep, but not tonight.

Hodgkin's disease. . . The prognosis ran around Nikki's tired mind as though she were being examined tomorrow. Even with the added symptom of night sweats, Luke's prognosis was good. If he'd been in remission for two years he was nearly out of danger. Nearly. . .

And then something hit her tired mind, making her sit up in bed and turn on her light. Hodgkin's disease. . . Treatment. . .

Was she right? Suddenly it was imperative that she know, and know right now. Now. . .

Padding softly through the darkened house, she found the text she wanted and returned to bed. Where was it. . .? Treatment of Hodgkin's. . . Diagnosis. . . Management. . . Chemotherapy. . .

What regime had they used? Nikki flicked the pages over, missing what she wanted in her urgency and having to return.

There were two chemotherapy regimes listed. The first was MOPP. . . Nikki stared blankly at the printed page. 'MOPP is associated with significant toxicity including infertility. . . MOPP therapy produces near-universal sterility in males. . .'

MOPP wasn't warranted, though. Not for stage 1B. The lesser regime was ABVD: 'Adriamycin, bleomycin, vinblastine and dacarbazine. . . Reduced risk of sterility. . . Recommended in stage 1B. . .'

Surely they'd used ABVD and not MOPP?

Even so. . . Even so, there was a strong chance that Luke Marriott was now sterile—that he would no longer be able to father children.

How would such an outcome hit a man who exuded masculinity as Luke Marriott did? To know that he could never father a child. . .

It was all just too hard. There was too much going on in Nikki's tired mind for her to assess what she had been told. Somehow her eyes managed to close and she fell into a troubled, dream-filled sleep.

She woke to laughter.

Nikki stirred, her eyes moving automatically to her bedside clock. It was close on seven, later than she usually woke, but in her exhausted, troubled state the night before she had not set the alarm.

The laughter sounded again, the high, tinkling sound of Amy having fun. For a moment Nikki frowned, thinking how rarely she had heard that sound lately. Why?

And then she heard a splash, and Nikki rose to her feet before she was aware she was doing so, her feet flying to the door. Amy wasn't allowed in the pool by herself. She knew the rules. It wasn't safe. . . She flung open the French windows, stepped through into the soft, morning sunlight, and stopped dead.

Amy wasn't alone in the pool. Luke Marriott was there too, his arms holding the laughing little girl high above the water and then swooping her down like a bird, so that her body flitted through the water and then swept up again, showering the man beneath her with sunlit water.

'Do it again,' Amy screamed. 'Do it again.' And Luke obliged, laughing with her.

Was this her daughter? Nikki put her hand to her eyes as if to rub the shreds of dreaming from them. Amy was a serious, grave little girl who seldom laughed. She took her life seriously, did Amy.

Or maybe that wasn't true. As Amy had been brought up in a house with an elderly housekeeper and a mother who distrusted the world, maybe there just weren't enough opportunities for laughter.

Amy looked up then and saw her mother. 'Look at me,' she screamed happily. 'Look at me, Mummy. Dr Luke's teaching me to dive. Look at me dive. Do it again, Dr Luke.'

Luke Marriott looked up at Nikki, his eyes quizzing her dangerously. 'Maybe your mummy had better go put on her swimming costume and join us. She'd be more respectable that way.'

With a gasp Nikki looked down. Her nightgown was a short, soft cotton one that was years old, and its age meant that it was almost transparently thin. And the sun was behind her! She put her hands up to cover her breasts and backed away.

'Mummy, do come in.' Amy's voice pleaded with her. 'Please, Mummy. We're having a really, really lot of fun.'

'Amy, I have to work,' Nikki said uncertainly. 'You and Luke are enjoying yourselves without me.'

'I always enjoy myself without you,' Amy said sadly. 'But if Dr Luke is here too. . .'

Oh, help. . . The tiny niggle of guilt which her daughter's laughter caused now rose to overwhelm her. 'I always enjoy myself without you'. . .

They were both watching her now—man and child. Amy was nestled in Luke's arms as though she belonged. She watched her mother with eyes that expected to be rebuffed. Luke's eyes gave away nothing.

'OK.' Nikki swallowed. 'I'll come in.'

She was rewarded instantly with Amy's whoop of joy. 'Yes!' she yelled. 'Mummy's coming in. Mummy's coming in! Hurry, Mummy. The water's beeyoootiful. . .' She arched back and plummeted her small body downwards, under water, and emerged, choking and laughing. 'We'll get Mummy in, won't we, Dr Luke?'

'It's your Mummy's decision,' Luke grinned. 'We have nothing to do with it.'

'Oh, yeah?' Nikki said to herself grimly, stalking in to find her bathing costume. This place had been sane before Luke Marriott arrived. The man was turning their lives upside-down.

Five minutes in the pool, she promised herself. A token to appease Amy. And then work!

Only of course it wasn't five minutes.

The morning sun was hot by the time Nikki slipped self-consciously into the water, and the water was a balm to her tired body. She had slept badly and was thick with bad dreams and self-doubt. Somehow the sun and the water and her daughter's laughter dispelled the black cloud. Luke was teaching Amy dead man's float, taking his duty very seriously. Nikki floated aimlessly on her back, watching man and child enjoy each other.

This was what Scott should be doing. Enjoying his daughter. Loving his daughter. Instead of which. . . She had written to him, but Scott had never even acknowledged that his little girl existed.

It was a bitter thought, but this morning it didn't seem as bitter as it usually did. Somehow the sting was eased.

Because Luke was here? The thought drifted around Nikki's mind as she floated, and she had to acknowledge that while Luke was here she had no place in her mind for Scott. For the first time Scott's face blurred in her mind, as though the memory was fading. The laughing eyes. . .the mocking smile. Where were they?

Gone with Scott. Replaced suddenly with eyes that laughed with a sympathy that was not feigned—that mocked, but mocked with kindness and compassion. She looked to where Luke was bending over the small, wet Amy, holding her still while the child tried desperately to keep her body floating. Kindness. . . This wasn't some errant playboy making a line for her. This was a man who genuinely wanted her small daughter to feel good about herself.

And then his eyes shifted to her and his smile faded a little. 'Feel better for your swim, Dr Russell?'

Nikki found her feet and stood upright, breast-deep in water.

'Thank you. I'd. . .I'd better be settling down to work. And. . .'

She was absurdly shy somehow, having trouble making her voice work. It was so. . .well, so darned domestic, to be in the water—the two of them with the child. 'And you'd better be thinking about morning surgery,' she managed.

'Not yet.' It was Beattie's voice cutting across the morning stillness. Nikki looked up to see the house-keeper smiling down at them. She was carrying a vast, loaded tray. 'Pancakes,' she called. 'I saw you out here and decided you might like a special breakfast.'

'Pancakes!' Amy surfaced from her float, still bub-bling with excitement. She looked from Luke to Nikki. 'Pancakes for breakfast! We haven't had pancakes for breakfast—ever.' She looked anxiously across at her mother as if expecting this treat to be somehow snatched away. 'Will you both stay to eat them?' The child was used to Nikki eating on the run. 'Please?'

'Of course we will,' Luke promised, holding out his hand to tow Amy to the side of the pool. 'Won't we, Nikki?' And he held out his other hand.

It would be churlish not to take his hand. Amy stared at her mother, waiting for Nikki to take the proffered hand. Nikki wavered helplessly.

'Come on, Dr Russell,' Luke said gently. 'Pancakes await us. And I'm not one to hesitate where pancakes are concerned. Are you?'

Still the hand was out. To avoid it Nikki had to walk right by, brushing him aside. Amy watched.

The sun was warm on her face. Nikki's body was cool in the water, but all of a sudden the water wasn't enough. It was as if she was flushing all over.

Slowly she brought up her hand. Luke's eyes were still, watchful, the laughter gone. In a slow, considered movement he brought his fingers closer and closed on hers. The three were entwined, man, woman and child.

'Come on, Amy,' Luke said slowly. 'Let's take your mother to breakfast.'

Somehow that morning Nikki managed a little study, but little was the operative word. Even with her contact lenses, her eyes refused to focus on the books, and when she forced herself to read the words aloud they failed to make sense.

What on earth was the matter with her? Amy was at kindergarten. Beattie was shopping and Luke was running morning surgery. She had the house to herself and she had less than three weeks to the exam.

'So work,' she muttered savagely. 'Make yourself work.'

She stared back at the page but all she saw was Luke—Luke lifting her daughter high in the air smiling up at Amy, smiling across at her. . .

'I'm going nuts,' Nikki whispered. 'I can't. . .'

Can't be falling in love? The words suddenly slammed into her head and stayed. Falling in love with Luke Marriott? What on earth was she thinking of?

'You just feel sorry for him,' she told herself

savagely. 'Because of the cancer. . .'

But that wasn't true at all. This morning the fact that Luke Marriott had suffered from Hodgkin's disease had been thrust away into some far recess of her mind. She hadn't been thinking of it while she had been in the pool.

All she had been thinking of was him. All she had been aware of was his body—his presence—binding her to her small daughter, entwining them into a threesome like a family. . .

Oh, good grief! She had to stop this. Luke Marriott was here for another few weeks and then he would be gone—forever. Just like Scott.

Not like Scott. Her mind suddenly rebelled, refusing to link the two men, and she stood abruptly. She was getting nowhere at all. If she went on like this she was going to fail this damned exam.

The phone cut across the silence and she answered it gratefully. Anything to get her mind away from these dangerous thoughts. It didn't help, though. It was Luke on the end of the line.

'Nikki, I'm seeing Sandra Mears at twelve,' he told her. 'I'd like you to be present.'

'But——'

'I know. I'm covering for you. But Sandra needs someone who's going to provide ongoing support. If I persuade her to trust me and then leave, she'll be no better off than before. I've done the groundwork, but I want you to be involved.'

So who was whose boss? Nikki held the receiver back and stared at it. She was used to giving the orders.

He was right, though. Her exam—her studying—was important, but not more important than the long-term happiness of the Mears family.

'I'll be there,' she told him slowly. 'What have you done so far?'

'I've another patient in the waiting-room,' he said

curtly. 'I can't talk now. But I'd like you here at twelve.'

Yes, sir. Nikki thought the words but wasn't given a chance to utter them. The line was dead.

CHAPTER SIX

BY THE time she reached the clinic, Nikki had worked herself up to anger. It was the only feeling she was capable of defining, and it covered a number of other emotions she was trying to dismiss.

Luke Marriott might have been ill but it hadn't stopped him being autocratic. He said jump and he expected the world to jump. He should have asked—not ordered.

Maybe I should dock his wages, Nikki thought humourlessly. On the grounds of insolence.

The thought gave her a fleeting ray of comfort, putting the relationship back on a purely professional basis. She climbed out of her little car, self-consciously smoothed down the next frock from Charlotte's never-ending supply, and made her way indoors. Her receptionist met her.

'Hi, Doctor,' Mary said happily. 'Wow, you look gorgeous.' She grinned. 'I don't blame you. Our new locum's worth dressing up for, isn't he?'

'I'm not dressing up for any locum,' Nikki snapped, but her receptionist simply arched her eyebrows and grinned.

'Mrs Mears is in with him now,' she smiled. 'The children are all over at the hospital. And I've cleared an hour if you need it.' She held up her fingers, showing them crossed. 'Good luck. Sandra's not going to take to interference very kindly.'

'She no longer has a choice,' Nikki said.

Sandra was sitting in an easy-chair in the surgery. Luke had come from behind the desk and was sitting beside her. They looked up as Nikki knocked and entered, Luke giving her a small, professional smile and Sandra looking downright scared.

'I asked Dr Russell to join us,' Luke said gently. 'I'm only here for another two and a half weeks and you'll need Nikki for longer than that.'

'Nikki'. . . The use of her name jolted her, and Nikki flashed Luke a look of annoyance before sitting. He didn't seem to notice.

'How's Karen?' he asked Sandra.

'She's fine.' Sandra's voice was apprehensive. 'At least. . .'

'Did you go and see her?'

'No.' Sandra shook her head defensively. 'I. . .I went and talked to the sister in charge. She says. . . she says Karen's OK.'

'Why didn't you go and see her?'

'She wouldn't want to see me.'

'I think she would.' Luke frowned. 'Sandra, what do you think Karen would say to you now if you went to see her?'

'Nothing.'

'Nothing? You mean, she wouldn't be upset that you hurt her?'

'No,' Sandra said bitterly. 'She'll just. . .she'll just look at me. . .'

'You'd like it better if she yelled at you?'

'Well. . .' Sandra's head sank down so that she was staring at the carpet. 'I. . .I hurt her.'

'So what are you going to do about it?' Luke's voice was unemotional and firm. It was as if he were asking what Sandra intended to have for dinner that night. That she should have something was as inevitable as the fact that she was now forced to take action.

Sandra raised tear-filled eyes. 'I don't know,' she said hopelessly. 'I don't. . .'

'Sandra, why are you living in that dump?' It wasn't a criticism, just a statement of fact, and Nikki's eyes flew to Luke. She would never have been so blunt.

'I. . .I can't afford anything else.'

'But you've the supporting mother's benefit. I've been on to the Department of Social Security here. They tell me what you get should cover one of the Housing Commission homes down near the river. They're basic but they're clean and well-kept—and with your skill as a housekeeper you'd get one looking great in no time. And they're right in town. The children could walk to school and you could walk to the shops.'

'But. . .'

'But what?'

Sandra swallowed. 'My husband. . .my husband ran up debts before he left. I'm paying them off but so far. . .so far I've done no more than cover the interest.'

'Does your husband pay any child support?'

For the first time Sandra's dark eyes flashed anger. It was as if something deep within her was hidden—and as though she was afraid of exposing her hatred.

'Of course not,' she said bitterly. 'He and his girl-friend are further south—he's a cane-cutter and makes a heap, but I'm left with nothing but his debts. His debts and the kids.'

Luke nodded. 'But you'd like some help?'

'I've no hope of getting it.' Sandra's voice flattened again. 'He spends as fast as he earns.'

'No.' Luke smiled then. 'The new rules require all employees—even casual workers—to register tax file numbers with employers wherever they work, and there's no way your husband can be working without doing that. All we have to do is ask Social Security to place a garnishee on his wages. You'll be paid before he is. And we'll ask for his debts to be transferred to his name. If you've sole responsibility for the children there should be no problem there.' He grinned. 'And he'll find his debtors have no trouble garnisheeing even more of his wages. Your husband might find himself with a little less easy money in the future, Mrs Mears.

And you might find things a whole lot easier.'

Sandra stared, hope and disbelief warring visibly in her tired eyes. 'If. . .if I lived in town I could sell the car. . .'

'That's right.'

'But——' Sandra swallowed '—folks around here think I'm a tart. Because I got pregnant before I was married. They'd give me a hard time. . .'

Nikki moved then. She rose and walked around the table. 'Sandra, there are lots like you in the town,' she said gently. 'Everyone has their ghosts. You can either move to a bigger city where you can be anonymous or stay here, look people in the eye and ride it out. You'll find history is forgotten as long as you act as though it's forgotten. Honest!'

Sandra looked up and smiled. 'You had a hard time too, didn't you, Doctor?'

'I sure did,' Nikki said ruefully. 'But I still wanted to stay. A small town has some good things going for it when it comes to raising children.' She touched Sandra's shoulder. 'And there are supports here that you won't find in the city. If you accept them.'

'I should have before this.' Sandra hesitated, looking from Luke to Nikki. 'If I'd admitted I was in trouble earlier, I could have got help. . .I wouldn't have hurt Karen maybe. . .'

'You're asking for help now,' Luke said gently. 'That's all that matters.' He rose as well, handing Sandra a slip of paper. 'The Housing Commission tells me there's a house vacant at the moment. Go and have a look before you commit yourself.'

'But. . .'

'But what?' He was smiling down at the girl, daring her with his eyes. 'This is going to take courage, Sandra. But you have it. I know it, and so does Karen.'

'Karen. . .'

He nodded. 'Your little girl has faith in you. You're all she has, Sandra.'

'Can I take her home?'

Luke shook his head. 'Not yet. You need time to sort yourself out, and Karen needs you at your best. Until you move you'll be worried and anxious, and that's the time when Karen is most likely to be at risk, isn't it?'

Sandra hung her head. 'Yes,' she whispered. 'But I wouldn't. . .'

'We can't risk that.' Luke's voice was firm. 'Karen doesn't need hospital but she does need care. I'm not fussed about involving community services and sending her to Cairns for foster care. I suggest that she spend the next couple of weeks with us at Whispering Palms.'

Nikki's eyes widened. She opened her mouth to protest but Luke's eyes were on her, hard and challenging.

'We have a great housekeeper, a comfortable bed and a little girl who'll enjoy your daughter's company. You can pop in and see her once a day, but you can have two weeks' time out from each other.' He smiled. 'It'll make you realise just how much you do care for your eldest daughter, and how much you risk losing if you don't put her first.'

'I don't risk losing——'

'Yes, you do.' Luke's smile faded. 'Sandra, if I reported this break to community services, they'd have no choice but to place Karen in foster care. Now, what we're offering is an alternative. Do you accept?'

Sandra looked wildly from Nikki to Luke and back again. 'But. . .but you don't want my daughter. She'll be a nuisance. . .'

'We'd love to have your daughter as our guest,' Luke said firmly. 'Whispering Palms is built for children, isn't it, Dr Russell?'

Nikki took a deep breath. She looked down at Sandra, and read the desperate need in her eyes. This woman had reaped a harvest more bitter than Nikki's from her relationship with her man. And Nikki could help. Luke was right.

'Whispering Palms is built for children,' she repeated slowly. She smiled at Sandra and her voice firmed. 'We'd love to have Karen.'

'You could have asked me!'

Nikki barely waited until Sandra had closed the door behind her before her anger burst forth. 'For heaven's sake, Luke Marriott, who do you think you are? It's my house!'

'And Karen needs it.'

'And you need it. And so does half the population of North Queensland, as far as I know. And you intend inviting them home. Home! My home. Not your home, Luke Marriott, my home!'

'Nikki Russell, do you know how extraordinarily beautiful you are when you're angry?'

Nikki slumped back into her chair and gazed up at the man before her in fulminating fury. 'If you think you can worm your way around me with your insincere compliments to get you what you want. . . You don't care, do you?'

'For your privacy?' He smiled. 'Not a lot. It seems you're taking enough care of that for both of us.'

'Just because I like keeping to myself——'

'And blocking the world out.' He shook his head. 'Nikki, Amy needs the rest of the world, even if you don't.'

'Luke Marriott, I am not your patient.'

'No?'

'No!'

'Well, then.' His smile deepened and he pulled his white coat from his shoulders, hanging it behind the door. 'If you're not my patient, then you can come to lunch with me. Hungry, Dr Russell?'

'No.'

'Liar,' he said equitably. 'Coming, or do I have to sling you over my shoulder and take you by force?'

'You wouldn't dare!'

Once more the irrepressible smile.

'Try me, Dr Russell. Maybe we'd both enjoy it.'

Nikki glared. Luke's smile didn't slip. She placed one foot tentatively forward and Luke's smile deepened even further. He would enjoy it, Nikki realised. He'd enjoy carrying her past her patients and receptionist with no thought at all for her dignity. . .with no thought for the fact that she was here forever in this town and had her reputation to consider.

'I'm going back to Whispering Palms for lunch,' she said half-heartedly, but he simply shook his head and took her hand.

'Beattie packed me enough lunch for three,' he told her. 'I want sea, sun, sandwiches and swim in that order. Let's go, Dr Russell.'

'I don't——'

'If you're worried about your precious virtue, you needn't worry,' he smiled. 'We're taking Karen.'

'Karen?' Nikki said blankly. 'But she's in hospital.'

'For the next three minutes,' he agreed. 'We're taking her to the beach for lunch and then you're taking her home to Whispering Palms.'

'Luke Marriott, do you have any idea what you're doing to me?' Regardless of listening ears on the other side of the door, Nikki's voice rose hysterically. 'I have exams in two and a half weeks. My house is filling with strangers. I never allow my work to impinge on my private life. To take a child home. . .'

'So what would you do, Dr Russell?' The hand holding Nikki's suddenly tightened, and Luke's smile slipped. 'Would you send Karen home to her mother before Sandra's been given a chance to sort her life out? Or would you put her on a plane to Cairns to be put into a foster home there? She knows you and she trusts you. Sandra can pop in and see her when she feels like it. . .'

'More people in my home!'

'Yes.' The smile crept back. 'With any luck, by the time I leave that place will start feeling like a home. Let's go, Dr Russell.'

Karen was still in bed when they reached the hospital, propped up by so many pillows that her wan little face all but disappeared. She didn't smile as they approached—just watched them gravely.

'How's my girl?' Luke smiled as he reached his small patient. His hand came down and ruffled the short, cropped hair. 'Feeling better?'

'Can I go home?' Karen's voice was lifeless and uninterested. Her eyes flicked over to the door as though she was expecting someone else to come.

'Karen, we're going to hold on to you a while longer.' Luke sank down to sit on the bed. He took Karen's small hand in his and his body blocked her view of the door. He looked down, silent until he was sure he had her full attention. 'Karen, your mum broke your arm, didn't she?'

The child stared up, silent, and Luke nodded.

'You don't have to tell us,' he said. 'But it's not you who needs the treatment—it's your mum.'

'You're taking her away. . .'

'No.' Luke's hands came up to grip Karen's slight shoulders. 'Karen, you've seen a balloon burst, haven't you? What's happening to your mother at the moment is very much like what happens when you blow a balloon up too far. She has so many worries—and each one is like a puff into a balloon. The worries build up and build up, until the last little puff makes her explode. That little puff might be just a child coughing at the wrong moment—or tea burning—or even just a draught from an open door. It's not the person who caused the tiny puff who's at fault, but the explosion comes just the same.'

'You mean. . .you mean when she gets angry. . .'

'I mean that's what happens when your mum hurts

you.' Luke's eyes didn't leave the child. 'Your dad
isn't giving your mum the money she needs to support
you. She can't afford to buy the food you need. The
littlies are causing her too much work. She's lonely
and she's worried and all these things are just building
up and building up to the point where she hurts you.
She feels dreadful about it, Karen.'

'But. . .'

'I know. She doesn't come. It's because she's
ashamed, Karen. Can you understand that?'

Karen's big eyes filled with tears. She looked wildly
up at Nikki, the doctor she knew and trusted. 'She
doesn't have to be ashamed. And she shouldn't be
worried. I can look after her. I try. . .'

'I know you do.' Nikki moved swiftly to give the
little girl a hard hug. 'But you've been trying on your
own for long enough. Now it's time for Dr Marriott
and me to take a turn. What your mum needs now is
a rest and a chance to sort herself out. So while she
does that she's agreed to let you come to stay with us
for a holiday.'

'Us?' Karen looked through her tears from Nikki to
Luke and then back again.

'Yes.' Nikki's voice firmed. She didn't look at Luke.
OK. He was right. This little girl needed Whispering
Palms more than Nikki needed her privacy. 'You know
Amy—my little girl—and Mrs Gilchrist. We've a
swimming-pool and lots of toys and books. Your arm
can heal while your mum finds a new place for you
to live.'

'A new place. . .?'

'Yes.' Luke grinned and pulled back Karen's covers.
'A perfectly splendid new home where you and your
mum and brothers and sister can all live happily ever
after. Now, Miss Mears, we have a picnic lunch to eat
and a quick swim before Dr Russell takes you to your
temporary accommodation.'

'But——' Karen looked up wildly '—I won't be able

to swim. I haven't got my bathers and. . .and you said I mustn't get my plaster wet.'

Luke shook his head solemnly. 'No problem.' He glanced around to the ward nurse. 'Sister here will provide us with a large plastic bag and a rubber band for your arm, and as for the rest—well, if you're wearing a plastic bag you can't be accused of skinny-dipping, can you?'

Karen looked from one doctor to another. Her tear-drenched eyes widened. And then, very softly, she giggled.

So what was happening to her nice, quiet study period? Nikki sat in her study and gazed out over the pool. Amy and Karen were sitting under the vast grape-vine discussing the merits of alternative ways of dressing Barbie dolls. It was evidently a very solemn topic—both little girls were taking the matter very seriously. Despite herself, Nikki smiled. It hadn't occurred to her to have children here to play with Amy, and now—now she saw how much pleasure Amy could get from it.

And Karen too. Karen had enjoyed her picnic to the full, laughing at Luke's silly jokes and thoroughly enjoying frolicking in the shallows with him. Later, though, as Nikki had tucked her into bed for an after-noon sleep, the shadows had come back over her face. 'I want to go home,' she'd whispered.

'Not yet, sweetheart,' Nikki had told her. How to tell a child that her mother was still so tense that she might strike her again? They couldn't risk it. Then, as tired tears had welled in Karen's eyes, Amy had appeared clutching her teddy and a battered stuffed monkey.

'I have to have an afternoon sleep too,' she'd announced. 'And I thought I could sleep with Karen if. . .if I let her use Monkey.'

It was the perfect solution. Karen had moved over

in the big bed and the two little girls cuddled down
together. They were asleep in minutes.

So Luke was right. Luke Marriott was always right,
Nikki had thought bitterly. He could organise everyone's life except his own.

She had picked up her abandoned text and stared
at it uselessly. She'd still been staring two hours later
when the sounds through the house had announced
that the girls were awake and ready for fun.

The exam was starting to seem irrelevant. So what
if I fail it? she'd asked herself, and then blinked. What
had she just said? She looked out of the window as
the two little girls emerged to the poolside. As she
watched, Beattie brought out a tray of lemonade and
biscuits. Nikki saw her glance doubtfully across to
Nikki's window. She'd be wondering whether to disturb her, Nikki knew, and suddenly Nikki threw her
text aside. It was time for a few minutes with the
children, she decided. Some things were more important than exams.

A few minutes? An hour and a half later Nikki was
still by the poolside. Amy's entire collection of dolls
was dressed to the young ladies' satisfaction and the
young ladies themselves were clothed in a variety of
evening wear supplied by Nikki. They looked amazing.
Both had high heels, stockings down around their
ankles, mock pearls and diamonds and enough make-
up to supply an entire chorus line. Luke arrived home
just as Nikki was lining up the giggling girls and
assorted dolls to be photographed for posterity.

'Wow,' he said reverently, emerging from the French
doors to the astounding sight. 'A real bevy of beauties.'

'We're gorgeous, Dr Luke,' Amy announced import-
antly. 'Aren't we?'

'You certainly are,' Luke grinned. He picked Amy
up and swung her high, causing her stockings to fall
down around his face. 'Ugh. What are these?'

'They're my pantyhose,' Amy said indignantly,

making a futile clutch as they fell. 'I don't know how Mummy keeps 'em up.'

'Mummy has hips,' Luke said, grinning wickedly across at Nikki. 'Ample hips is what you need, my girl.'

'Are Mummy's ample?'

'They certainly are.'

Nikki gasped. Without thinking she abandoned her camera, scooped down and brought up a huge handful of pool water, directing it straight at Luke. It hit him full in the face.

Karen's jaw dropped but Amy crowed in delight. 'Yay, Mum,' she yelled. 'Do it again.'

'I'm not sure I could,' Nikki said nervously, backing away from the pool.

Luke grinned. He picked up a towel and carefully wiped his face. His shirt-front and tie were sodden.

'Mummy growls at me when I get my clothes wet,' Amy giggled. 'Are you going to growl at Mummy?'

'Of course I am,' Luke said severely. He frowned direfully down at the two children. 'What do you think I should do to her?'

'Nothing,' Karen said nervously, but Amy was made of sterner stuff.

'I think she should be spiff. . .spifflicated,' she pronounced.

'Oh, yes?' Luke's straight face broke. 'And what exactly is spifflication?'

'I'm not sure,' Amy confessed. 'I think. . .I think it's sort of like tickling.'

Luke grinned. 'I can do that,' he agreed. He turned back to Nikki. 'Prepare to be spifflicated, Dr Russell.'

'Don't you touch me——'

'In front of the children,' Luke finished for her smoothly. 'Of course not. You have your dignity to maintain. I only ever spifflicate in private. Beattie!'

The housekeeper appeared from nowhere. She had obviously missed nothing of the proceedings. 'Yes?'

Beattie Gilchrist was close to laughter, fighting to keep a straight face.

'Is dinner something that will spoil?'

'It's casserole, Dr Luke.'

'Would it ruin your day if I told you I was taking Dr Russell off to dinner and hence to a fate of spifflication?'

Beattie chuckled delightedly. 'Of course not,' she beamed. 'The casserole will taste better than ever tomorrow night, and me and the girls will cook ourselves hamburgers. You won't mind, will you, girls?'

'No way,' Amy shouted, but Karen looked troubled. Luke crossed to the little girl and knelt down.

'What is it, Karen?' he asked gently.

'You won't. . .you won't hurt Dr Russell, will you?' the child asked tremulously. 'She didn't mean to get you wet.'

'Don't you believe it. Our Dr Russell did so mean to get me wet.' Luke took Karen's hands in his and gave them a reassuring squeeze. 'But no, Karen. I may tickle Dr Russell until she screams for mercy but I won't hurt her. Not now. Not ever. I don't hurt people. That's a promise.'

The laughter had gone from his voice. He met the little girl's eyes, and what she read in his seemed to reassure her. The corners of her mouth struggled to smile. 'I like hamburgers,' she said simply.

'Then that's settled.' Luke turned to Nikki. 'Go and get yourself into a pretty dress, Dr Russell. I'll take off one sodden shirt and then. . .then prepare to meet your doom!'

'But I like hamburgers too,' Nikki said weakly. This was going too fast for her. She had no intention of going out to dinner with this man.

'Beattie, if you were doomed to spifflication, where would you want to eat your last meal?' Luke demanded, ignoring Nikki's protest and turning to the housekeeper.

Beattie chuckled. 'Only one place to eat out here-abouts,' she told him. 'The fishing co-op runs a club. The dining-room looks out over the harbour. It's real pretty and the food's not bad either.'

'It sounds just what the doctor ordered,' Luke smiled. 'OK, Dr Russell. You have ten minutes to prepare yourself. Let's go.'

The man was like a bulldozer, Nikki thought grimly. She stood in her bedroom and gazed helplessly at the mirror. A meal out. . . To be taken out by a man. . .

To be taken out by Luke Marriott! Nikki closed her eyes as a wave of confusion ran through her. What was happening? She should be staying at home study-ing. She should put her hands on her not so ample hips and tell Luke Marriott exactly what she thought of him.

If he hadn't been ill, she would do, she decided, but it was hardly fair when he'd been through such a bad time.

'That's not the reason and you know it,' she told her reflection out loud. 'You want to go out.'

No, you don't, a little voice inside her protested.

'Yes, you do.'

Nikki thought back to Luke Marriott kneeling before the troubled Karen, and a feeling of warmth flooded over her. This man was kind and caring and. . .

This man was trouble. Capital T. Trouble.

He would be gone in a couple of weeks. He was transient—a transient presence in a life which so far hadn't been all that much fun.

'Why shouldn't I go out, then?' Nikki demanded of her reflection. 'Seize the day. Live for the moment.'

You're talking rubbish! that inner voice asserted.

'Oh, leave me alone!' Nikki turned her back on her wiser self and stared into the wardrobe. She had hung the clothes Charlotte had sent her and then ignored all that she could. Now she crossed to pull the racks apart.

Charlotte was never a girl to do things by halves. She

had taken Nikki's wardrobe as a personal challenge, omitting nothing.

And there was something just right for tonight. Something just right for a first and last date. A night to forget she was Dr Nikki Russell who took the world seriously. A night to forget the loneliness of the rest of her life. . . Taking a deep breath, Nikki slipped the fabric over her shoulders.

The dress was soft white silk, loose-fitting but clinging with the sheerness of the fabric. It hung low across her breasts, the soft sleeves cut away so that they exposed her slender arms. The dress fell in delicate folds around her thighs and down to swirl around her long legs. A ribbon of palest green looped around the waist and down to hint at its presence among the folds as she moved.

The dress turned her into someone she wasn't. Or someone she had once been but had forgotten existed. Nikki stood before the mirror and stared. Unconsciously she brought her hand up to gather her hair into a loose, curling knot of flame. The action made her seem younger, and more vulnerable. She let it fall, and then in swift decision put it up again. Before she had time to change her mind she pinned it and turned from the mirror. She had done it. She was ready.

'Wow!' It was Amy, bursting through the door, her new friend tagging behind. 'Wow, Mummy, you're beautiful. Isn't she beautiful, Karen?'

'My mum's prettier,' Karen said stoutly. 'But. . .but you're really pretty, Dr Russell.'

'Is she ever!' Luke Marriott was standing in the passage. He too had changed, into a dark suit which made Nikki see just why he had caused so many problems among the nursing staff in the city. Drop-dead handsome, the man was. She looked up, blushed and looked away again. What on earth was she doing?

'Have a really good time, now,' Amy ordered them. 'What time will you be home?'

'By midnight, Mother,' Nikki laughed, swooping her small daughter up to give her a kiss. 'Don't wait up for me.'

'Don't spifflicate her too hard, will you, Dr Luke?' Amy warned.

'I make no promises,' Luke grinned. His arm came around Nikki in a proprietorial gesture. 'Vengeance is mine, Dr Russell. For tonight, you're at my mercy.'

CHAPTER SEVEN

IF THERE was to be only one evening left in the world, this could well be the evening. It was a night to forget the past, forget the future and just be.

Something had snapped inside Nikki's controlled head. Who knew what had caused it? Was it the culmination of long years of work and worry, Charlotte's lovely dress floating around her slim form, the balmy tropical night, or the presence of the man at her side—a man whose smile made her heart do crazy jumps inside her body and made her forget that she was Dr Nikki Russell with the weight of the world on her shoulders? Which of these things was causing the feeling of euphoria creeping over her? Nikki didn't know, and she no longer cared. The night was hers.

And somehow for Luke it seemed the same. The world was put on hold. They were alone together and nothing else mattered.

Miraculously there was a table available in the best part of the club—a sheltered alcove with windows looking out over the lights of the harbour to the sea beyond. The waiter showed them to their seats with an astonished second look at the town's transformed lady doctor. I didn't know you existed, his glance said, and Luke's hand tightened on Nikki's waist as he guided her forward.

The lady's mine for the night, his hand said. Keep off. Nikki should have shrugged the hand aside but she wouldn't. Not tonight.

Afterwards Nikki couldn't remember a thing they'd talked about. Inconsequential nonsense, she suspected. Luke kept her in a ripple of laughter as they ate. The tiny pieces of calamary still tasted of the sea, and of the lemon groves in the hills above the town—and the grilled whiting melted in Nikki's mouth, blending in with her perfect night.

He made her seem the most desirable woman in the world, Nikki thought, and wondered fleetingly how many other women had been given the same treatment. It didn't matter. Not tonight. Tonight was hers.

They ate huge red strawberries and farm-fresh cream, drank their coffee and then rose reluctantly to leave. Miraculously the beeper in Luke's pocket stayed silent. It was as if the world were holding its breath.

'A walk, I think,' Luke told her as they emerged to the star-filled night. 'I'm not ready for bed yet, Dr Russell, and I don't think you are either.'

'N-no.' It was true. Nikki didn't want this evening to end. In the morning she would be back with her books, and Luke would be back to being her locum, and the world would have shifted on to its rightful axis. But not yet. . . So they walked along the sand, barefoot, with shoes dangling in their free hands. One hand of each was in use, linked unconsciously with the other.

They walked far from the lights of the jetty and of the town, around the headland where the beach stretched out for mile upon endless mile of deserted sand. The moonlight played on their faces. From somewhere a long way off Nikki heard herself talking of her childhood—telling this man things she had told no one—of a lonely childhood with eccentric parents in a house too big for her—but with love and laughter always present. And Luke talked too—a little—of his family in Melbourne and his life before. . .before he knew he had cancer.

It was as if the last few years were taboo. They weren't spoken of. The night was magical, and ugly realities weren't allowed to intrude.

And finally their wandering feet came to a halt and Nikki's voice fell silent. Luke let his shoes drop to the sand, removed Nikki's sandals from her grasp and then took her shoulders, turning her to face him in the moonlight.

'So what now, my lovely Nikki?' he said softly. 'Are you going to let the world in again? Is your life going to have ended when Scott walked out the door?'

'I don't. . .'

'You can't let that happen,' he told her, his fingers tightening on her shoulders. 'I'm pushing you hard, but when I go, will you close the door on life again? Retire back into your parents' house and shut the world out?'

'When I go'. . . The words hung between them and Nikki was aware of a rush of desolation sweeping through her. This was a transient thing. This moment was just what she knew it must be—a dream—a fantasy of something that could never be.

'It's none of your business what I do when you go,' she managed to whisper.

'But it is.' His hands came up to cup her cheeks. Tilting her face, he looked deeply into her troubled eyes. 'I care about you, Nikki.'

'Yes, you care,' she agreed bitterly. 'The way you care about Karen. And the way you care about Sandra. Like all the other waifs you've decided to adopt as part of your healing process.'

It was unfair. Nikki's accusation was contemptible and she knew it, but somehow. . .somehow it was so important that she be different.

And she was. She saw it in the sudden blaze of anger in Luke's deep eyes and the tightening of his mouth. His hands held her harder.

'Why do you do this?' he said softly, his voice dangerously low. 'Why do you want to lash out at me?'

'I don't. . .' Nikki's voice fell away. 'I don't know,' she whispered miserably. 'I'm sorry, Luke. . .'

Her words trailed away. Between them there was a long silence, broken only by the rush of the sea in its constant washing of the vast stretch of beach.

Luke gave a low, savage moan and turned to stare out to sea. Nikki's hands came up to touch her face where he had held it. What now? What?

And then slowly, as though driven by something he didn't understand and couldn't fight, Luke turned. He reached out to take her face again, and when she tried to pull away his hands gripped harder. For a long, long moment he stood looking down into her bewildered face, and then, infinitely slowly, he stooped to kiss her.

It was a harsh, demanding kiss. It was a kiss of confusion and pain, and of punishment. You've hurt me, the kiss said, and I take my revenge. . .

But then it was more than that. The lips that demanded possession of her mouth were asking something more than appeasement of anger.

They wanted her. They wanted to know her mouth—know the secrets of her tongue—possess the smooth contours of her even teeth. They wanted. . .

It wasn't the lips that wanted. It was the man. And the woman wanted in return. Nikki felt the hardness of Luke's body against hers, and a flame started deep within her. This was a sweetness that she had never known. She could smell him, taste him, feel him, and she wanted more! She wanted to be closer than she had ever been to a man in her life before.

Where were the memories of her long-gone husband? They were certainly not here. In fact they no longer existed—blown away by the sensation of these hands holding her, these fingers caressing the smooth contours of her thighs, pulling her closer to feel the urgency of his want—his need.

'Luke. . .'

She wasn't sure that she whispered the name aloud but it crowded her consciousness. It was a cry of desperate loneliness, need, and the start of some crazy hope. Soon this man would be gone, but if only. . .if only. . .

It didn't matter. For tonight there were the stars and the sea and this man holding her as if she were the most precious thing in the world. Nikki arched herself against him and felt his head drop to her breast.

Somehow the loose silk of her dress was put aside and Luke's mouth covered the taut wanting of her nipples. The sensation was so sweet that Nikki cried aloud and tears of joy coursed down her face.

Oh, God, it had never been like this with Scott. She had thought Scott was a friend and he turned into her husband. This man, though. . .this man was no friend. This man was her mate—her soulmate—her love. . .

Her love. The word swept through and through her and she knew with absolute certainty that it was true. She loved Luke Marriott with every ounce of her being.

She loved. She loves. She will love. Forever and ever and ever. And then as Luke's arms came around her, cradled her and gently lowered her to lie on the warm sand beside him, she knew that whatever he wanted was right with her. If he only wanted her for this moment, then this moment would have to last forever.

And then, from some far-away place, came the sound of a harsh, electronic beep. It grew into a crescendo, splitting the night with its awful insistence. Luke's mouth stilled where he had been exploring the valley between her breasts. As Nikki grew rigid in his arms, he swore unsteadily and rose.

'Fate worse than death,' he said unsteadily. 'I think we're wanted, my love.' He put down a hand and pulled her to her feet, his arm pulling her to his body. Kissing her roughly on the mouth, he put her from him in bitter resolution. 'The world calls. Let's see what they have to say.'

'The world calls'. . . Nikki stood, confused, as Luke searched his trouser pocket for the beeper. He lifted it high to see its faint light in the moonlight.

'McDonald baby arriving,' he read. 'Assistance required.'

'McDonald. . .' Nikki frowned. 'But. . .but Mrs McDonald's only seven months pregnant.' She thought back to the last time she had seen Lara McDonald. Last week. And she was only twenty-nine weeks then. . .

'I'll have to go fast,' she said unsteadily. 'We'll have to try to stop labour until we get her to Cairns.' She was already searching in the sand for her sandals.

'We'll walk faster without shoes,' Luke told her. 'Come on. Ready for a run, my love?'

They covered the distance back to the car in a time Nikki would have thought was impossible. Luke, however, was in a hurry, and with his hand holding hers anything was possible. He gave Nikki's feet wings. It was a desperate run, with both knowing the need for urgency, but somehow. . .somehow it was still part of the magic night. Whatever the night held, Nikki was as one with Luke Marriott. If he ran fast then she was part of him, carried along by emotion.

She was gasping for breath as they neared the car, but as Luke stopped to find the key she started laughing.

'I feel like a naughty child trying to get home before they find I'm missing,' she laughed. 'Oh, Luke, I hope we can stop this labour.'

He looked down at her curiously in the dim light, and his mouth twisted into an answering smile.

'So do I,' he murmured. 'But whatever we do, we need to do it fast.'

It was an enigmatic statement which Nikki didn't follow. There was no need to say the obvious, she thought, but then they were in the car, with Luke's hand on the horn as they turned back out on to the main road towards the hospital.

Nikki turned her face towards the ribbon of bitumen, forcing her thoughts savagely away from the man beside her. Lara McDonald didn't need a love-struck girl, she needed a competent doctor, and that was just what Nikki had to be.

Nikki was out of the car almost before it had come to a halt at the front door of the hospital, running swiftly up the tiled steps and through the glass doors. The night sister came out to meet her.

'She's in the labour ward,' the sister said. Behind her, a big man in denim work trousers and generous flannelette shirt materialised out of the shadows. He was literally wringing his hands, but ceased momentarily as he reached to clutch Nikki's arm.

'The baby'll die if it comes now,' he said hoarsely. 'Doc Russell, it's too early. And Lara's had three miscarriages already. This. . .this is our last chance——' He broke off to run his hand across his wet cheeks. 'Oh, God, Doc, you gotta stop it. If this baby doesn't make it. . .'

'Sister, could you find Mr McDonald a cup of strong, sweet tea?' Nikki said. 'And then come straight back to the ward. Have you examined Mrs McDonald?'

'I didn't like to,' the sister told her. 'I thought I might make matters worse.'

'Good.' The nurse was right. An internal examination might hurry things even further. She turned to the labour ward and found Luke by her side.

Two doctors. . . At least there were two doctors. If the baby was born it would have a much better chance if it could have the undivided attention of Luke while Nikki attended the mother. She smiled gratefully up at Luke as he swung the door wide.

Lara McDonald was a small, wiry woman in her late thirties. She and her husband owned a small sugar farm just out of town, and struggled to make ends meet. Lara's face reflected it, weathered and lined from years of too much sun and hard work.

Her face was further lined now, creased in agony as a spasm ripped through her. Her eyes were wide with terror, and as Nikki approached she reached out to clutch her hand.

'Stop it,' she whispered frantically. 'You've got to stop it.'

Nikki kept hold of the hand until the worst of the spasm passed. Out of the corner of her eye she could see Luke scrubbing and getting into gown and gloves. Once more she was grateful for two doctors. It meant she could stay where she was.

'Let's not panic,' she said gently. 'Wait until we see what's going on. When did you start having pains?'

'After dinner. About. . .about an hour ago?'

'Have you had a show? Any bleeding?'

'No.' A fresh spasm hit and the hand clutched again.

Then Luke was at the table. The night sister had returned, and together she and Nikki lifted away Lara's cotton dress. Nikki frowned as the fabric fell to the side. Lara was mid-spasm but her swollen abdomen was smooth and still. Nikki put a hand on the firm flesh. Nothing. This wasn't a contraction.

She looked a question to Luke. Swiftly he performed a gentle examination, his face clearing as he did.

'There's no dilation at all,' he told Nikki. 'Mrs McDonald, what did you have for dinner?'

'I. . .' Lara was wincing through pain. 'I don't. . .' Then she paused. 'Curry,' she said suddenly. 'We had curry.'

'Do you often have curry?' Luke's voice was clipped and professional, demanding the woman's attention.

'No. . .' She managed a faint smile. 'But. . .but I really wanted it. So Bill went down to Innisfail to get some for me. He got three tubs. . .'

Luke grinned. 'And you ate the lot.'

'Well, Bill didn't like it.'

Luke shook his head. Nikki found herself relaxing, the tension oozing out of her. Three tubs of curry when unaccustomed to it. . .

'Mrs McDonald, you're not in labour,' she said

gently. 'I'm sure of it. What's happening to you is caused by your system reacting to curry. Probably your pregnancy has made you a bit more prone to tummy upsets than usual, and the curry is making itself felt.'

'Is that all?' The woman's eyes widened. She stared wildly from Nikki to Luke and then back to Nikki. Slowly the frantic terror behind her eyes faded. Still clutching her stomach, she fell back on to the pillows, exhausted. 'Oh, my God,' she whispered fervently. 'Oh, thank you.'

'Any time.' Nikki grinned. She looked up to see Luke's smile reflecting her own. Relief was making her light-headed, she thought suddenly. She felt like singing. Or maybe. . .maybe it wasn't all relief.

'We'll give you an injection to settle your tummy, and we'll keep you overnight,' Nikki reassured her patient, forcing her attention away from Luke. 'But you'll live to eat curry again.'

'And. . .and the baby. . .?'

'It seems he's enjoying the new sensations you've been causing him too much to want to leave,' Luke grinned. 'I bet he emerges in two months demanding more vindaloo and chapattis.'

'Ugh. . .' Lara McDonald moaned. 'Don't even mention them. . .'

A few minutes later they left their patient resigned to an uncomfortable night. Nikki had kept a straight face as she'd administered medication, but as she climbed into the car she broke into delighted chuckles. It wasn't often that dramas turned so nicely into farce.

'Unsympathetic wench,' Luke growled. 'Did you never have food cravings in pregnancy?'

'I was desperate for oysters and beer one night,' Nikki confessed. 'But I made myself a cup of hot milk instead.'

'A very restrained young lady,' Luke nodded. His hand came over to her side of the car. Starting from the tip of her knee, his fingers gradually worked their way upwards. 'Keep your eyes on the road, Dr Russell,' he advised kindly. 'Just remember how restrained you are.'

Nikki gasped. 'Don't. . .'

'Why?' The fingers were touching the soft flesh of her inner thigh through the flimsy fabric of her dress. 'Why stop, Dr Russell?'

'Because I'll crash the car if you don't,' Nikki managed.

He grinned. 'Point taken. How long until we get to Whispering Palms?'

The house was in darkness when they arrived home. A solitary lamp burned in the hall, but Beattie and the children had long gone to bed. Nikki locked the big front door behind them and then turned uncertainly to the man beside her. All of a sudden she felt very young, and very shy.

'G-goodnight, then,' she stammered.

He flicked her cheek with his finger, lifting an errant wisp of flaming hair. 'Do you want it to be goodnight, my Nikki?'

Of course she did. Of course she wanted to walk along the passage to the solitude of her own room. She could even do an hour's study before she slept.

So why was she slowly shaking her head, as if mesmerised by Luke's slow smile—the look of understanding and care in his hypnotic eyes? Hypnotic. . . It was the right word, she thought ruefully. It was as if she were drugged. Her eyes held his and she smiled uncertainly up at him.

'N-no.'

'Are you sure?' He took her shoulders in his hands and held her at arm's length. 'Nikki, I make no promises about tomorrow. I'm here for two and a half weeks and after that. . .well, after that, who knows where I'll be? But for now. . .'

She could hardly accuse him of deceiving her. He was laying his bitter cards out for her to see, and if she didn't like them she could leave right now—walk through the house to her bedroom and close the door hard behind her.

But he wasn't lying. This man was telling her the truth, and, no matter how unpalatable it was, the truth was what she wanted. Scott's lies and deception had been with her for too long for her to want anything else.

And she wanted Luke. His eyes held her, mesmerised, and Nikki knew that if two weeks of this man was all she could have, then two weeks would have to be enough. It would have to suffice for the rest of her life.

She lifted her hands to hold his face, and stood on tiptoe to touch his lips with hers. 'If tonight is all we have,' she whispered, 'then tonight is all there is.'

For a long moment he stood motionless. Nikki felt a moment's searing panic. She had thrown herself at him. Would he react in disgust?

And then his hands came around her body, and tenderly she was lifted up to lie cradled in his arms. He held her hard against him and his lips deepened the kiss.

'My bedroom has the double bed,' Nikki whispered as the kiss came finally to its sweet end, and Luke chuckled.

'Ever the practical one, Dr Russell.' He pushed the door from the hall open with his foot. 'Well, Dr Russell, what are we waiting for?'

It was the sweetest night Nikki had ever known.

Five long years she had been without a man, and her body had forgotten just how good it was. Or maybe her body had never known. Luke held her tenderly in his arms and the world was forgotten. All she knew was the feel of his skin against hers, his warmth embracing her, making her feel the most desirable woman in the world.

And when tenderness turned to urgency it was Nikki's desperate need that drove her on. She wanted this man so much. She wanted to be closer to him than she had ever been to another person in her life before. She wanted to be part of him, one with him, and when they climaxed together she soared on a pinnacle of ecstasy that made her feel the night was exploding around her.

Oh, God, she loved him. She loved him so much. . .

Nikki drifted towards sleep in his arms, his face cradled in the rise of her breasts, and her heart swelled in a rush of pure tenderness. She would do anything for this man. Anything. And he was only hers for two and a half weeks.

They hadn't taken precautions. Nikki's eyes suddenly widened in the dark as the thought struck. Suppose. . . Suppose she was wrong about Luke's infertility. . .?

He felt her sudden stiffness, and stirred to lift her face to his. 'What is it, my beautiful Nikki?' he asked sleepily.

'Luke. . .' Nikki said unsteadily. 'Luke, I'm not. . .I'm not protected. I didn't think. . .'

'There's no need.' Luke's voice was suddenly bitter. 'You know the ramifications of the treatment for Hodgkin's disease as well as I do, Dr Russell, and as for anything else. . .well, I haven't been with a woman since I was ill. You're quite safe.'

'Oh, Luke, I'm sorry.' Nikki could have bitten her tongue from her head.

'Yeah, well, leave it,' Luke said roughly. 'Go to sleep.'

She didn't straight away. As Luke slept, Nikki lay in the dark and tried to come to terms with what she was feeling. She couldn't. The emotions crowding through her mind were those she had never felt before and had no idea how to cope with.

'I haven't been with a woman since I was ill. . .' Where had he been? Had he moved from locum position to locum position since then? And if so, what was he trying to escape?

It was too much. For now, he was here and she could somehow assuage the barrenness of the past. And he could do the same for her.

Nikki nestled her head against Luke's bare chest. He stirred slightly in his sleep and pulled her closer.

She slept.

Luke woke at dawn. Gently he disengaged himself from Nikki's arms, but the slight movement woke her. For a moment—just a moment—she wondered where she was, and then the tender memories flooded back. Her hands reached out to hold him to her. He couldn't leave. Not yet.

'It's nearly morning.' Luke smiled tenderly, leaning over to kiss the smooth skin behind her ear. He entwined a golden curl in his finger and then replaced it reluctantly where it had been lying on the pillow. 'Do you want your daughter to burst in on her not so respectable mama, Dr Russell?'

Nikki chuckled and her hands tightened. Luke's chest was broad and muscled and warm. A tremor went through her as the flame started to spread without volition through her naked body. 'Amy's a heavy sleeper,' she whispered. 'And she's under strict instructions not to wake Mummy until seven.'

Luke shifted slightly so that he could bring his arm up from under Nikki's supine form. 'Give me back my watch, woman,' he growled. Finally he held it up. 'Six-fifteen,' he announced. 'That gives us forty-five minutes.'

'Forty-five minutes for what?' Nikki asked breathlessly. She knew, but to ask was heaven.

'If you don't know, then I'm not the man to tell you,' Luke told her sternly. He moved to pull his body up and over her. The flame in Nikki's thighs was building to an inferno.

'You. . .you won't tell me?' she managed.

'Lady, what use is talking?' he muttered. He leaned down to take first one nipple and then the other between his strong teeth. It was all Nikki could do to stop herself crying aloud. 'What use is telling, when I can show you?'

CHAPTER EIGHT

LUKE left her with five minutes to spare.

Luckily Amy chose this morning to sleep late, so Nikki was able to shower and pull her disordered mind back into some sort of control before her daughter and their visitor burst in.

'Luke's in the swimming-pool,' Amy informed her. 'Beattie says we can swim too, but will you come as well?' Then she frowned at her mother. 'You look different.'

'I wore this dress a couple of days ago,' Nikki said self-consciously. It was one that Charlotte had sent. 'Don't you like it?'

'I remember. It's a pretty dress,' Amy agreed. She eyed her mother up and down. 'It's not that that's different. It's. . .' She stopped. 'I don't know what it is.'

'Your mum's smiley,' Karen announced suddenly. 'She's not usually smiley.'

'Well, I hope your mum's smiley today too,' Nikki said softly, stooping to give Karen a swift hug. The hug did more than show affection to the little girl. It also enabled Nikki to hide her mounting colour. 'She's coming to see you today, and maybe she'll take you for a walk to show you your new house.'

'Will I go back home today?'

'We'll get you moved into your new house first,' Nikki promised. 'Karen, it might be a week or two before your mum's got things under control. Do you think you can put up with us for that long?'

Karen nodded solemnly. 'I like it here,' she said seriously. 'And if you think Mum needs a rest. . .'

'I think you both need a rest,' Nikki told her. 'When

your arm's a bit better and you can go back to being
your mum's best helper then we'll send you home so
fast we won't see you for dust. Faster than a speeding
bullet. . .'

'Faster even than Superman. . .' Amy giggled. 'I like
having Karen here. Mummy, are you coming swimming with Luke?'

Nikki shook her head. 'No.' She dared not. The
thought of Luke in the swimming-pool. . . The thought
of Luke anywhere at all was enough to turn her knees
to water. She needed strong black coffee and some
distance between them. 'You girls go,' she ordered.

'But Luke's waiting!'

'Let him wait!'

Once again they breakfasted by the side of the pool.
Whispering Palms was transformed, Nikki thought
fleetingly as the children's laughter sounded across the
water. Beattie was beaming and affable. She kept looking from Luke to Nikki and back again, and Nikki
knew exactly what was in her mind.

'You need to find yourself a nice new man,' Beattie
had told Nikki over and over again, and now, seem-
ingly, one had found her cherished Dr Nikki. And such
a nice young man! Beattie handed out extra pancakes
and her smile broadened.

'Are you staying home to study all day?' Beattie
asked Nikki, refilling her coffee-cup, and Nikki
nodded.

'Though I'll have to go in to the hospital first,' she
told the housekeeper. She was carefully avoiding
Luke's eyes. 'I need to check Mrs McDonald.'

'I can do that,' Luke told her lazily.

'No.' Nikki flushed and stared intently at her cup
of coffee. 'Lara's my midwifery patient and I should
see her.'

'Suits me.' To her surprise Luke didn't argue. He
pushed back his chair. 'Thanks for breakfast, Beattie.'

He lifted his brows at Nikki. 'Coming, then?'

He could as well have kissed her. His eyes smiled at Nikki as he moved to help her rise and she felt herself flush to the core of her being. She felt beautiful and desirable and. . .and loved. Oh, if only she were. . .

There was a minor hiccup. Luke had been using Nikki's car and Beattie needed the house car to take the girls to school and kindergarten. 'It's no problem,' Luke told her as Nikki voiced doubts. 'I'll drop you back after the hospital rounds. You'll still be home in time for enough study to suit your rigid requirements.'

Nikki looked up at him suspiciously but he wasn't laughing. He wouldn't laugh at her, she thought suddenly. He'd laugh with her maybe, but not at her.

They found Lara McDonald perched up in bed eyeing her breakfast dubiously. 'Do you think I should?' she asked as Nikki and Luke entered.

Luke grinned. 'I don't see why not, do you, Dr Russell?'

'Not too much,' Nikki advised. She crossed to the bed. 'Feeling better, then?'

'A hundred per cent.' Mrs McDonald took a deep breath. 'You know, maybe some of the pain was just fear. I thought the baby was coming and it got worse.'

'It happens.' Nikki lifted the chart and smiled at what she saw. 'Everything's fine, then. I see no reason why your husband can't take you home this afternoon. Stay until after lunch, though. We'll see how your tummy responds to breakfast first.'

'He won't want me home.' The woman smiled shyly. 'He cossets me that much! If he had his way I'd stay in hospital for the next two months.' She sighed. 'I can't blame him. This baby means so much to both of us.'

'I know,' Nikki said gently.

'Well, maybe you don't,' the woman said. 'You had

your baby young, if I remember right. My husband
and I, though—well, we've been trying for ten years.
Ten years is a lot of time to be without a baby when
you really want one.' She bit her lip. 'I don't know how
people cope when they can't have children. I think. . .I
think I might have gone mad.'

'Or maybe you would have found the strength to
cope,' Nikki said gently, trying hard not to look up at
Luke. 'There's more to life than having children.'

'You say that, but then you have your daughter,'
Lara said firmly. 'And maybe I'll say that when
I've got my brood safely round me. But not until
then.'

A slight sound made Nikki turn. Luke had quietly
left while the woman talked, closing the door
behind him.

'Oh,' the woman in the bed said. 'He's gone. I guess
he's in a hurry and I was wasting your time with my
small talk.' She looked up at Nikki. 'Such a nice man,'
she smiled.

'Yes,' said Nikki dully. 'Such a nice man.'

There was little else for Nikki to do. All the other
patients in the hospital had been handed over to Luke.
She spent ten minutes in the office going through cor-
respondence and then made her way back out to the
car. Luke appeared fifteen minutes later.

'There should be a taxi service in this town,' Nikki
said lightly as he lowered himself into the car beside
her. For once, Luke's face was set and grim. Nikki
turned away, not wanting to see the etching of pain
in the lines around his eyes.

'It's no problem to drive you back.'

'No. But it'll make you late for surgery.'

'Will you dock my pay if I'm late?' Luke demanded,
and Nikki swung back towards him, surprised by the
intensity of his tone.

'Don't be daft.'

He laughed without humour. 'It's happened before. Being a locum is the pits.'

'So why do you do it?'

Luke's mouth tightened even further. He swung the little car out of the car park and was silent for the rest of the drive home.

That was the last time they talked for the day. Back at Whispering Palms, Nikki left the car without a word. For the life of her she couldn't think of a thing to say. Tackle what's really wrong, her medical training told her. Probe the hurt. And yet. . . And yet this was the man she loved and she couldn't do it. She couldn't hurt him further.

She spent the rest of the day desultorily studying, but to her surprise she achieved a lot. 'I'm in danger of passing this blasted exam,' she told her reflection as she dressed for dinner. 'Which makes Luke Marriott's arrival well worth while.'

The thought held no comfort at all. Nikki stared bleakly at her reflection and then turned away. What on earth was happening to her nice ordered life? She had no idea.

Luke wasn't in his customary position in the kitchen when she appeared. Beattie shook her head disapprovingly at Nikki's questioning look. 'He won't be in,' she said tightly. 'Rang and said he had a case out the other side of town. It's only Verity Birchip. I told him if he spent his life running all the way out to Birchips for every one of Verity's imaginary ills he'd have his work cut out for him, but he wouldn't listen. Said he'd grab something to eat in town and be home late.'

'Maybe there really is something wrong with Verity,' Nikki said mildly.

'That'll be the day,' Beattie snorted. 'You mark my words—Verity Birchip'll go to her grave swearing she has something the medical textbooks haven't even heard of and demanding to know why the heck the doctors are worrying about her dying of old age when she's got something far more interesting.'

Nikki managed a chuckle and Beattie looked at her closely.

'What's the matter, then, lass?'

'Nothing.' Nikki crossed to the cutlery drawer to avoid Beattie's penetrating gaze.

'Something is. And it wouldn't be why Dr Luke had suddenly decided to spend tonight out, would it?'

'Beattie Gilchrist, you're out of line!'

'You'd say that to your own mother.' Beattie crossed her arms and fixed Nikki with a look. 'And it's your substitute mother talking now. Nikki Russell, if you play your cards right——'

'Beattie, be quiet.' Nikki clapped her hands on her ears and glared at her housekeeper. If only Beattie knew that Nikki was playing every card she had—and it wasn't going to be enough.

There was a long silence, and then, thankfully, the door burst open and two small girls tore in.

'We're starving,' Amy said breathlessly. 'Mummy, where's Dr Luke?'

'He's out on a call,' Nikki told her abruptly, stooping to kiss her small daughter. She smiled down at Karen. 'How was your day, Karen?'

'Good,' the little girl said seriously. She appeared to consider the question. 'Mummy picked me up after school and took me around to see the house she's been offered. We think. . .' Despite her solemn tone the child's face suddenly twisted into a smile. 'We think it will be satisfactory. It has one bedroom for Mummy, one for the girls, one for the boys and. . .and one left over. And it's nice! It's even got an inside toilet!'

'That's great.' Nikki swooped to give Karen a hard hug. 'And when does Mummy think she might be able to move?'

'The lady at the hospital has offered to look after the littlies.' Karen was back to being solemn—an eight-year-old matron. 'Mummy says it will take her a week to have everything sorted out. She said if I was able to help she'd be much faster, and she really misses me.' Karen looked up anxiously. 'She said she's really sorry she hurt me. She said she was so worried she went a bit crazy, but you and Dr Luke are fixing it up so she'll never get like that again. She cried, and she hugged me and. . . I. . .I don't think she'll do it again.'

'I don't think she will either,' Nikki told her, with a small rush of relief. Sandra was talking to her child. The lines of communication were open and, by the sound of it, Karen still considered them friends. Sandra was still only twenty-two and her relationship with her daughter might always be more one of friendship than mother-daughter—but then, that was OK too.

'Can I go home when she's moved in?'

'Of course you can, sweetheart,' Nikki assured her, and made herself a promise to contact Sandra the next day. By the look of things the situation was improving rapidly, but it needed to.

It was a long night. Nikki read the girls to sleep, and then went back to her study. Every time a car came up the road she let her book fall as she listened, but it was close to midnight when Luke finally came home. Nikki listened to the brisk tread of steps along the hall and then his bedroom door closing firmly behind him.

She was being shut out. Whatever intimacy had existed between them last night had ceased to exist now.

She prepared herself for bed and climbed between cool sheets in her lonely bed. Last night Luke had been here. Last night. . . The memory of him was all around her and he was so close. . .

The night was hot. Above her head the wooden ceiling fan lazily stirred the air but it wasn't enough. Nikki tossed and turned as she struggled for sleep, but it wasn't forthcoming.

Finally she could bear it no longer. She slipped out

of bed and padded along the bare wooden boards of the hall. Her naked feet made no sound.

There was a light shining underneath Luke's door. Nikki hesitated for a moment and then, taking a deep breath, softly knocked.

Silence. Had he gone to sleep with the light on? Then, as she turned reluctantly away, afraid to go further, the door opened inwards.

Luke was still fully clothed. He had been working. The desk behind him was strewn with papers, and a pen had been tossed hastily aside. All this Nikki saw before Luke moved to block her view.

'What is it?' he asked abruptly, and Nikki flinched.

'I. . .I couldn't sleep.'

He looked down at her for a long moment, his eyes inscrutable as he took in her slim form scantily clad in her wispy cotton nightdress. 'I dare say you have sleeping-tablets in your bag,' he said roughly at last.

Nikki drew in her breath. 'I don't need a sleeping-tablet,' she managed angrily. 'I need to talk.'

'What about?'

'Luke Marriott, what the hell is going on?' Despite her struggle for dignity and control, Nikki's voice rose. Her words echoed down the darkened corridor and instinctively she looked towards the door behind which the children slept. 'Luke, can I come in?'

'No.'

'Why the hell not?' Suddenly Nikki's fragile hold on her temper snapped. 'What are you playing at? Last night you treated me as the most desirable woman you knew and tonight. . .tonight you don't even want to talk to me. What have I done to deserve being treated like a one-night stand?'

Her voice was a whisper, intense, angry and wavering. To her fury she felt hot tears slip down her cheeks, and she brushed them away angrily with her hand.

Behind them she heard the sound of a child stir in her sleep and cough. Nikki winced. Luke stood before her, implacable and immovable. Remote.

'Damn you, Luke Marriott,' she whispered brokenly, and turned away.

He moved then. In two swift strides he caught her, seized her shoulders and swung her round to face him.

Away from the light of the open door Nikki couldn't make out his expression. Not that she looked. She was aware that her body was trembling as she tried to stay rigid in his grasp.

'Hell,' he muttered savagely.

'It is,' Nikki whispered. 'Maybe you'd better let me go, Luke.'

'Nikki. . .'

The child coughed again and Luke swore. Seizing Nikki's hand, he pulled her forward into his bedroom and closed the door behind him.

Silence stretched out between them. Within the small room, Luke released her. Nikki stood numbly against the closed door, her hand idly rubbing her arm. There would be bruising there where he had pulled her.

'God, Nikki, I'm sorry.'

The words were wrung from him. Nikki looked up at him, her eyes dull and heavy. 'For making love to me?' she asked flatly.

'I never meant to.'

'No.' She kept rubbing her arm as if by doing so she could assuage some of the hurt in her heart. 'I don't suppose you did. Charlotte said. . .'

'Charlotte?'

'My friend in Cairns. She said you couldn't help yourself where. . .where women were concerned.'

'God, Nikki, last night was different.' He turned away, his voice agonised. 'I'd say that anyway, wouldn't I?'

'Yes.'

'It's the truth.' He turned back to her and grasped her shoulders. 'It's the truth but it still can't make a difference to the final outcome. The truth is that I was mad. I forgot. . . I don't want you, Nikki. I don't want a woman. Not now. Not ever.'

'That's not how it felt last night.'

'No. But last night. . .last night I was crazy. Just for a little. . .'

'You forgot that you can't father a child?' Nikki took a deep breath. 'Is that what it is, Luke?'

'No. Yes.' He thrust her back from him. 'God, Nikki, you're so lovely. You stand there and all I want to do is make love to you and. . .'

'And what?' Nikki said gently. 'Luke, you accused me of shutting the world out. Aren't you doing the same thing?'

'Leave it, Nikki,' he said roughly.

'No.' Nikki shook her head, her red-gold hair tossing from side to side. 'You've hauled me from my splendid isolation and now. . .now you're telling me I'm really alone after all.'

'You're not alone. You have your daughter. . . Beattie. . .this town. . .'

'Oh, yes. That's not what you said a week ago.'

'Nikki, it doesn't matter.' Luke's eyes hardened. 'Whatever I said, whatever I've done doesn't alter the fact that I want no one. I should never have made love to you, because, of course, you want more. . .'

Nikki's green eyes flashed. She took a deep breath. 'You arrogant toad!' she spat.

'I meant. . .' He rubbed his hand wearily through his hair. 'Nikki, I didn't mean that to sound. . .I just mean that lovemaking implies emotional commitment and I can't give that. Not now. Not ever.'

'Not ever'. The phrase echoed harshly around them. Nikki took a ragged breath and leaned against the door. At least he was honest. Last night. . . Last night she had thought it would be enough. Now. . . Now she hated his damned honesty.

She hated him. He was avoiding the issue. Running. Just like her father. Just like Scott. . .

So what was left? Their professional relationship. She could tell him to get out of her house now—or somehow she could act professional. One doctor to another. . .

'How was Mrs Birchip?' she asked suddenly.

'Mrs Birchip?' Luke looked blank.

'The lady you spent the night with.'

'I beg your pardon?'

'You did a house call to Verity Birchip,' Nikki said coldly, striving desperately for a return to normality. 'And it kept you all night.'

'Oh.' Luke's blank look suddenly faded and he managed a smile. 'Mrs Birchip thinks she has heredity.'

'Heredity?' It was Nikki's turn to sound blank.

'She read somewhere that heredity can cause all sorts of problems, so she thinks she's got it. I suspected a bad cold, but she's sure it's heredity.'

'You know, I wouldn't be the least bit surprise if she's right,' Nikki said slowly. 'It would explain a lot.'

And Luke managed to grin. 'Yeah. . .'

So this was all there was. Over. A fine romance, Nikki thought bitterly. Gone the way of all the loves in her life. Walking away from her.

Nikki drew in her breath. 'I guess. . .I guess I'd better go to bed, then.'

'I think you should,' Luke said gently. His smile faded. 'Nikki, I'm sorry.'

'Don't.' It was practically a cry. She bit her lip and then gestured to the pile of papers on his desk. 'I'm. . .I'm sorry I interrupted you. What. . .what were you doing?'

'I'm writing a newspaper column.'

Nikki's eyes widened. 'A news. . . What sort of newspaper column?'

'"Who Cares?"'

'"Who Cares?"' Nikki stared in amazement. In disbelief she crossed to the desk and stared down. There were loose sheaves of handwritten pleas for help, and attached to each was a neatly written paragraph. Nikki picked up and read the first note.

Dear Doctor,
   My fifteen-year-old daughter has one breast bigger than the other and I can't get her to agree to visit our family doctor. I know she's scared stiff she'll be like this forever. . .

Then there was the response, carefully worded under the major heading 'Who Cares?'.

And Nikki didn't have to read the response. She had read 'Who Cares?' every week for the past eighteen months with a growing sense of admiration for the measured, careful and caring responses given by the anonymous answering doctor. She knew just what the reply would be—a careful reassurance, amusing anecdotes of 'lopsided adolescents I have known' as well as a plea to back up the reassurance by a visit to the girl's own doctor.

Nikki let the sheaf of papers fall to the table. 'You're the doctor behind "Who Cares?",' she whispered. She stared. This was making less and less sense. The column must pay well. Why then was he doing locums?

'Yes.' He came abruptly forward and pushed the papers into a folder. 'I started doing it while I was ill.'

'For the money?'

He laughed without humour. 'You guessed it. And besides. . .'

'It's a job you can do without people.'

'Nikki, I'm not trying to avoid people.'

'Only involvement.'

'Look who's talking.'

'You still think I'm trying to avoid involvement?' Nikki demanded. She put her hand wearily to her eyes. 'I think. . .I think I'm cured.'

He looked hard at her then, his eyes narrowing. 'Nikki, I——'

'You don't want to hear,' Nikki finished for him. 'Well, you're going to. You came up here for God knows what reason, but whatever your motive you decided on a nice, Boy Scout objective. Get Dr Russell out of herself. Involve her with the human race again. Teach her to love.'

'Nikki, I didn't mean——'

'I don't care what you meant.' Tears welled up in Nikki's eyes and she turned away. 'And I don't care what you were trying to do. All I know is that I love you. . .'

There. The words were said. She could do no more. This man was all she wanted in life and she had laid her heart on a plate for him to take. If he wanted it. . .

It seemed he didn't. He stood motionless for a long moment and then came to turn her gently towards him. 'Nikki, don't,' he said gently.

'Cry? Why the hell not? Isn't falling in love with yet another man who doesn't want me something to cry about?' She wrenched back away from him, her fingers searching for the doorknob while she watched his face. It was bleak and hard. Whatever she said would make no difference.

'Nikki, I'm sorry,' he said softly. Implacably. There was no love for her in the words.

'I'll bet you are,' Nikki whispered. She shrugged. 'And so am I.'

Her fingers found the knob and twisted. Nikki turned and walked out of the room. Regardless of sleeping children and housekeeper, she slammed the door. Hard.

She hadn't stalked more than three feet from the door when the front doorbell rang.

Nikki stopped dead. Now what?

Her hand flew up to her tear-stained face. Great. If she was needed now. . .

Luke's bedroom door opened again as he too heard the bell. 'I'll go,' he said roughly. 'You'd better wash your face and pull yourself together.'

Great. Professional caring and sympathy. And to make it worse he was right. Nikki watched him stride along the passage and if she'd had something in her hand she would have thrown it. Something hard and big, she thought savagely. Something that would break into a million fragments and release some of the awful tension within her.

Instead of which she went meekly back into her bedroom to repair some of the ravages of the last few minutes.

She had hardly started before Luke was back. His knock on her door showed as little respect as Nikki had for the still sleeping occupants of the house.

'Nikki, I need you.'

Like hell you do, Nikki thought bitterly. You don't need anyone, Luke Marriott. She didn't say it, though. Instead she let her robe slip to the floor, hauled on the dress she'd been wearing that afternoon and opened the door. 'What's wrong?'

He narrowed his eyes. 'Are you fit to operate?'

'Of course.' Nikki's hands were fumbling to fasten the front buttons on her dress, and once again she cursed fate at having sent Luke to stay in this house. She was forced to be intimate in such surroundings.

'We've a nasty tear and fracture to repair A fisherman got his hand caught in a cray-pot rope. It's darn near torn off his thumb.'

Nikki nodded. It happened. The fishermen worked fast and often didn't stop the motor when they dropped the pots. Occasionally one fouled on a propeller. There had been a couple of nasty accidents since Nikki had started practising.

'I usually send them down to Cairns,' she said quietly, trying to make her voice sound professional and detached. 'I can't. . .I don't have the skills. . .'

'I do.' He was striding away. 'Ring the hospital and

tell them to prepare Theatre. Then come. I'll drive him down.'

'He's here?' Nikki's eyes widened.

'He's currently making a mess of Beattie's hall,' Luke said grimly. 'His mates were set on a night prawn-ing and wouldn't interrupt to take him to the hospital. They dropped him at the wharf and he walked up here because Whispering Palms is closer than the hospital.'

'Good grief.' Nikki frowned in disbelief.

'Hurry,' Luke told her, turning away. 'The kid's lost a lot of blood and the thumb's hanging by a thread. The faster we get it sewn back, the more chance he has of keeping it.'

'The kid. . .'

'He's not much more than a teenager. . .'

It was a fiddly, delicate operation. Once more Eurong was in luck having Luke as acting locum, Nikki thought reflectively, knowing that if the boy had been sent to Cairns his thumb would have been well and truly dead by the time they got him there.

As it was he had a good chance of keeping it. Luke meticulously cleaned the shattered bone, inserted a tiny metal pin which would hold the bones together and then slowly stitched the mass of torn muscle and flesh back into the shape of a thumb. He used skills Nikki could only wonder at.

It took hours. The first trace of dawn was showing through the big south window of the operating theatre as Luke finally raised his head.

'That's it,' he said wearily. 'The best we can do.' He moved to adjust the intravenous line. It was feeding antibiotics through, which hopefully would keep the wound free of infection. Infection now would mean all their work was wasted.

It was considerate of Luke to include Nikki in his assessment of what had been done, but the work had been Luke's. Nikki's job as anaesthetist had been relatively easy, keeping a fit and healthy nineteen-year-old asleep for the time it had taken.

'Well done,' she said softly to Luke, signalling one of the nurses to assist him with his gown. He looked exhausted, and Nikki suddenly remembered that the man had been ill himself. Was he completely recovered?

'Is Mr Payne here yet?' she asked the charge sister. Jim Payne had given permission for himself to be operated on—at nineteen he was able to do so—and in response to their enquiries he had replied that his dad didn't give a stuff anyway. Beneath her hands the boy stirred as he took over his own breathing.

'Not as far as I know,' Andrea told Nikki. 'We telephoned home but no one answered. I guess his dad will still be at sea.'

Luke frowned down at the boy. 'Does he have any other family?' He had been scrubbing while Nikki had questioned the boy earlier.

'Only his father here,' Nikki said grimly. 'His father owns the boat Jim works on. He would have been the one to put Jim off last night.'

'With instructions to walk to hospital.' Luke stared down at their still sleeping patient. The boy was pale beneath his weathered complexion. At nineteen he still looked very young—and very vulnerable. 'Some people don't deserve to have children,' he said softly.

'No.' Nikki shook her head. 'There are some cases where parents can't seem to help mistreating their children—like Sandra Mears. It's just the build-up of hardship that proves too much for them. But Bert Payne's different. . . He's always been rough and uncaring. Jim's mum took off when Bert's roughness finally got too much for her, and since then Jim's had to cope with it alone.'

Luke's mouth twisted into a grimace. 'Poor bloody kid,' he said softly. 'I've given him back his thumb, but what sort of chance does he have?'

'He'll survive,' the nurse told them. 'The Paynes are tough.'

'Yeah. And toughness breeds toughness. Next generation. . .'

'Well, maybe he'll marry a nice girl who gives him all the cuddles he's missed out on,' Nikki said roundly.

'Ah, yes. The happy ending.' There was no mistaking the derision behind Luke's words and Nikki flushed.

'I'll finish up here,' she said tightly. 'You're tired.'

'Feeling sorry for me, Dr Russell?'

Nikki's eyes flew up to his and flashed fire.

'No,' she said between her teeth. 'I just want to get rid of you.'

CHAPTER NINE

THE days that followed were endless. Somehow Nikki managed to study but afterwards she never knew how. It was a defence mechanism, she thought dully. Immersed in her texts, telling herself they were important, somehow she could block out Luke's presence in the house.

Not that he was there often. He worked longer hours than he needed to, and Nikki suspected that many house calls were simply an excuse to be away from Whispering Palms. Away from her. . .

'I don't know what's eating the man,' Beattie puzzled one day as they ate yet another dinner without him. 'He was so darned cheerful when he came—like a breath of fresh air through the place—and now. . .'

'He's like a bear with a sore head,' Amy announced. 'Isn't he, Karen?'

Karen nodded solemnly and then carefully replaced her knife and fork on the plate. 'Mummy says she'd like me to come home on Saturday,' she announced. 'She says. . . she says the house is ready. She says it's really pretty and we've got a nice garden I can help look after and. . .'

'What else will she let you help with?' Beattie said darkly and Karen flushed, hearing the implied criticism.

'I like gardening,' she said in a small voice. 'I want to grow carrots. And. . .and flowers. And Mummy says I can. . .'

'I'll drop in tomorrow and see your new house,' Nikki intervened, sending her housekeeper a dark look. 'And if your mum's really ready, then I don't see any reason why you can't go home.'

*   *   *

It was yet another way of blocking her thoughts from
Luke—and no way was entirely successful. After lunch
the next day Nikki walked around the river to Sandra's
new home. It was quite a distance and by the time she
arrived Nikki was regretting her impulse to leave the
car at home. Especially as she rounded the corner and
saw her own second vehicle parked outside. Luke. . .

Oh, no! She stood irresolute in the sun as she tried
to decide what to do. The last thing she wanted was
to walk in on Luke. . .

Then the door opened and Sandra saw her. Before
she could move, Sandra lifted an arm and waved. 'Dr
Russell. Hi! Come and see.'

So there was nothing for it but to cross the road and
enter the sparkling clean home. Luke had obviously
just been leaving. He was standing in the hall as Nikki
entered.

'Two doctors,' Sandra said, smiling nervously. 'Do
I get charged for two house calls?'

'Of course not.' Nikki tried desperately to ignore
Luke as she smiled reassuringly at Sandra. 'I just
thought I'd drop in for a look.'

'Let me show you——' Sandra started eagerly, but
Luke interrupted.

'I have to be getting back for afternoon surgery,' he
told them. He didn't look at Nikki. 'I'll leave you
two alone.'

Sandra nodded. She looked up at him and then suddenly stretched out her hands to take his. 'I don't know
how to thank you,' she told him. She turned to Nikki.
'Did you know Dr Luke has located my husband?'
She whirled suddenly into the kitchen and returned
carrying a slip of paper. 'And look! I don't know how
he did it but it's a cheque. For child maintenance. And
they say. . .they say there'll be more coming.'

'It wasn't me that found him,' Luke told her. 'It was
the Department of Social Security.'

'I've been to them before,' Sandra said darkly. 'And

nothing's happened. And then you two move in and. . .'

'And your husband gets to shoulder his responsibilities,' Nikki said warmly. 'I'm so glad.'

Sandra smiled. For the first time in years she seemed young. 'This will mean—oh, everything. We'll have enough to eat for a change, and there'll be money left over. I'll be able to buy them new clothes, and take them to the pictures sometimes.' She giggled. 'And my husband. . .he's not going to have all that great a time with his new girlfriend now,' she chuckled. 'Not with his wages being garnished for maintenance for the kids. Plus,' she ended triumphantly, 'all the stuff he bought on credit cards and I've been paying off. Some of it he's still got and the rest he's sold. His girlfriend was there when the social welfare people came around and she told them without thinking, "Oh, yeah, he bought that. . . That old stereo," she said, "he sold it," and things like that. And they told the credit people and the credit people transferred the debt. I don't get to use the credit cards any more but I never did anyway. So now. . .so now he's got to pay for the lot and I don't have a single debt. I feel. . .I feel fantastic.'

'Ready for Karen?' Nikki said quietly.

Sandra's smile faded. She met Nikki's look without flinching. 'I'm ready for Karen,' she said. 'I think. . .I think I've come to terms with what I've been doing with her. I just felt so darned useless. . . And Karen's so like me. So when I felt like punishing myself I took everything out on her.' She took a deep breath. 'But it won't happen any more, I promise you that. Karen. . . well, Karen's going to be a little girl again. And I'm going to be a proper mother.'

'You know there won't be any more chances,' Luke said heavily. 'You know that, don't you, Sandra?'

Sandra nodded. 'I know you two have given me a second chance,' she agreed. 'I know that and I'll be grateful forever. And I won't mess it up.'

'Karen can come back to Whispering Palms at any time,' Nikki promised. 'Use us as a safety-valve. If you feel the tension's mounting then send her to us.'

'To us'. . . Because she was standing beside Luke it sounded as if the invitation was from both of them and Sandra took it as such. She smiled at both of them in turn.

'I'll take you up on that if I ever need to,' she promised. 'But I won't. I know that now.' Suddenly she leaned forward and kissed Nikki on the cheek. 'And Dr Russell?'

'Yes?' Nikki was flustered and it showed in her mounting colour.

'I'm really glad you've been given a second chance too.'

Luke left them then, much to Nikki's relief, and Sandra showed her around the house. It looked lovely. Finally Sandra walked her to the refrigerator and opened the door. The interior was crammed with the sort of food most children would die for—lemonade, cocktail sausages, chocolate éclairs, lamingtons. . .

A small boy sidled up beside Sandra as they looked and pulled his thumb from his mouth to announce, 'No one's allowed to eat anything until Karen comes home. It's Karen's welcome-home party 'cos we're glad she's better and we missed her. Mummy's put me in charge of seeing no one cheats.'

And this was the little boy who'd triggered the scene that had ended with Karen's broken arm. Nikki smiled down at him and wondered just how she'd react, given the scenario of not having enough food to feed her children. She looked back to Sandra and saw that Sandra guessed her thoughts.

'It tore me apart,' she whispered. 'To be hungry myself and still watch Karen be hungry—and for her not to complain. . .'

'It won't happen again,' Nikki said softly. 'It's over.'

'I know.' Sandra smiled happily. 'And guess what?

I've got a spare room and Dr Luke suggested I might take in a boarder. It'll mean even more money, and I'll have someone—some adult—to talk to.' She grimaced. 'I know I've been treating Karen too much like an adult—but then, I've needed to. I've been so darned lonely.'

'I know the feeling,' Nikki said softly, and their eyes linked in a moment of understanding. And Nikki knew in that moment that Sandra would ask for help if she needed it. There was a bond between them which both recognised.

Nikki left then, her heart a little lighter because of the family's obvious happiness. She glanced at her watch as the door closed behind her. It would take her half an hour to walk home, which left her with a solid afternoon to study. On Sunday—in two days' time—she had to climb on to an aeroplane and face the exam in Cairns.

It no longer had meaning. It was a meaningless milestone she was aiming for because she had nothing else to do. Nothing but face a future which was bleak and empty.

'I still have Amy,' she said aloud. 'And Beattie. And Whispering Palms. And a good job.'

And it sounded empty. There was a void that only Luke could fill.

She looked up towards the road and her heart stilled. Her car was parked on the corner. Luke was waiting.

He got out of the car as she approached, and watched her walk towards him.

'I thought you were late for surgery,' she said nervously.

'So sack me.'

She shook her head, and unbidden tears threatened behind her eyes. 'You know. . .you know I wouldn't.'

He shrugged. 'I thought you could do with a ride, seeing as I'm using your car. It's bloody stupid walking so far in the midday sun.'

'I know,' Nikki said bitterly. 'I'm bloody stupid.'

He glanced over at her as he started the car, and his mouth tightened. It was as if he was agreeing with her.

'You leave for Cairns on Sunday,' he said evenly.

'Yes.'

'Your exams are on Monday and Tuesday.'

'Yes.' She couldn't think of anything further to say.

'And you'll be back here on Wednesday.'

She nodded, unable to trust her voice.

'I'll leave here first thing Thursday, then.'

'Fine.' She hardly recognised her voice. It was tight, young and forlorn. She sounded about Amy's age, lost, desolate and alone.

Once more he glanced at her and then stared determinedly back at the road. 'It's better this way,' he said finally.

'Why?' It was all she could do to whisper. 'Where. . .where are you going?'

'I'm not sure. Maybe I'll go back to Sydney for a while. Spend some more time on my column.'

'Fine.' She couldn't think of anything else to say. Instead Nikki sat with her hands clenched tight in her lap and waited to be deposited home.

There was little more preparation she could do for the exam. If she didn't know what she needed now, she never would. Nikki desultorily packed and stared aimlessly at her books for the rest of the weekend. On Saturday she took Karen home to be welcomed by a tearful Sandra and her joyful brothers and sister, but that was the only cheerful spot in the day.

'When you get back there'll be no Karen and no Dr Luke,' Amy said dolefully as she hugged her mother goodbye on Sunday. 'Mummy, what are we going to do?'

'We survived fine by ourselves,' Nikki told her daughter, forcing a smile.

'But we weren't happy,' Amy reminded her. 'Dr
Luke makes me laugh.'

He doesn't make me laugh, Nikki said to herself sadly.
She clenched a tight wad of paper in her hand—a
note left on the kitchen table when Luke had left this
morning on one of his interminable house calls.

'Good luck,' the note read. 'Love, Luke.'

'Love. . . . You don't know what love is,' Nikki whispered to the absent Luke as she made her farewells.
'You have it. If you want it, it's yours. . .'

Nikki stayed in the staff residence of the hospital while
she sat her exams. It was the same hospital she'd stayed
in the night she'd come down with her two casualties.
She took the opportunity of visiting them and her
spirits lifted a little as she found both recovering well.

'It's the last time I drive a car fast,' Martin told her
and Lisa, settled in a wheelchair beside Martin's bed,
agreed with him.

'I was egging him on,' she said sadly. 'We were fools.
Lucky fools.'

'At least you're both alive to learn a lesson from it,'
Nikki smiled. The pair were now inseparable, their
hands linked tight while they talked. A happy ending
if ever she saw one.

And she was so jealous she could cry. Nikki turned
from the bed as her friend Charlotte came into
the ward.

'Oho.' Charlie grinned. 'Back in town. Need some
more clothes, do we, Dr Russell?'

'No, I do not.' Despite her cross tone Nikki couldn't
suppress a smile. Charlotte was incorrigible.

'So it's just exams that's brought you to town. How
boring. I suppose I can't persuade you to join me for
dinner tonight?'

'Are you kidding?' Nikki linked arms with her friend
and they walked out together. 'My last night before
the exam. . .'

'And this exam is so important!'

'It is to me.'

Charlotte shook her head. She glanced across at Nikki's strained face and wisely decided to hold her peace.

'Would you have half an hour to spare from your hectic exam preparation, though?' she asked slowly.

'Charlotte, I can't. . .'

'Not to spend in riotous living,' her friend assured her drily. 'But there's someone in town who badly wants to see you.'

'Who?'

'Luke Marriott's sister.'

'Luke's sister.' Nikki turned and stared at her friend. 'What on earth. . .? Why would Luke's sister want to see me?'

'I suspect to ask after Luke.'

'But. . .'

'Look, don't ask me.' Charlotte spread her hands. 'I'm only the intermediary. I only know that this girl's from Melbourne. She told me about Luke's illness— apparently she hasn't seen him since then. She's worried sick about him and came north to try and locate him. I heard she was asking the staff if anyone had heard from him—I stuck my oar in and told her where he was and I told her you were coming down. She was due to fly back to Melbourne today but has held over to try and talk to you. Will you see her?'

Nikki frowned. 'I suppose so.'

'So what's the story?' Charlotte linked arms again and kept walking. 'Has he murdered someone?'

'Who? Luke Marriott?' Nikki tried to laugh. 'I wouldn't think so.'

'So why's he running?'

'Who knows?' Nikki said lightly, much more lightly than she felt. 'Who knows?'

*   *   *

Luke's sister, Megan, was a more petite version
of Luke, in a feminine form. She was blonde, blue-
eyed and beautiful, and her smile would turn men's
hearts. Her smile was tentative when she met Nikki,
as though she was afraid of what she might be about
to hear.

'I hope you don't mind me bothering you,' she
started awkwardly as Nikki ushered her into her sparsely furnished little bedroom an hour later. 'Miss Cain
says you have exams tomorrow.'

'It doesn't matter.' Nikki pulled out the hard chair
from the desk, motioned her guest into it and then
perched on the bed. 'How may I help you?' They were
both so nervous, the air was brittle, she thought.

'I thought. . .I just wondered if you could tell me
about Luke.' The girl gripped her hands together and
held them hard. 'We. . .we were so worried. My company sent me up here for a conference and I thought
I'd try to find out about him while I was here.'

'You haven't heard from him for a while?'

'No.' Megan bit her lip. 'Oh, we heard about his
illness. He rang from Sydney and my oldest sister flew
up to be with him during the worst of it. But then. . .
then he just seemed to withdraw. Since he left Sydney
we've received the occasional postcard from different
places and nothing else. It's as if. . .it's as if he doesn't
want us any more.'

Join the club, Nikki thought bitterly, but she didn't
say it. Instead she looked sympathetically across to
Megan. The girl was young, maybe only twenty or so,
and looked miserable.

'You're fond of your brother?' she asked.

'We all are.' The girl took a deep breath. 'We're a
really big family, Dr Russell. I'm the second youngest
of eight children and Luke is the oldest. My father
died when I was two and my mum died three years
ago. Luke. . .well, Luke's been more a parent than a
big brother. . .to all of us.' She looked at the floor.

'We know he's not working—at least, until I heard
about you I didn't think he was. My young brother's
still at university, though, and the cheques keep
arriving from Luke to keep him there. I don't know
how he's doing it.'

Nikki did. This explained why he had to do the
locum work. But. . .

'But why doesn't he contact you?' Nikki was talking
almost to herself.

'We. . .we wondered if he was still ill. If his cancer
had come back. If he didn't want to face us?'

Nikki shook her head. 'It hasn't,' she said gently.
'He's fit and healthy and I'd be willing to bet he's
going to be one of the lucky ones who's in for a
complete cure.'

'And is he happy?' Megan asked tremulously. 'It's
driving us crazy not knowing. Last Christmas. . .well,
we all got together—all of us and husbands and wives
and children—do you know that Luke now has eleven
nieces and nephews with two more on the way? And
the only one not there was Luke. The only one. And
you know——' she lifted a woebegone face '—I would
have said, of all of us, to Luke the family was the most
important.'

And maybe it still is, Nikki thought slowly. Maybe
the sight of his brothers and sisters marrying and pro-
ducing their own families when he can't is just too
painful for him to face.

She didn't say that. She couldn't. Instead Nikki
leaned forward and gripped Megan's hands.

'Megan, I can't answer your questions,' she said
gently. 'I don't know the answers myself. All I can do
is assure you that Luke seems healthy. If you like I'll
tell him I've seen you, and tell him you're worried.
That's. . .that's all I can do.'

'But he is at Eurong?' Megan's tear-stained eyes met
Nikki's. 'I can't extend my stay now, but one of my
brothers or sisters will come up. I know they will.' She

grimaced. 'Maybe if you don't tell him we're coming. . .'

'Megan, he won't be there.'

Megan paused. 'N-no?'

'No. Luke's doing a locum for me and he leaves on Thursday. And I don't know where he's going.'

Something in her tone caught Megan's attention. She stared. 'You. . .you care for him too,' she said slowly.

Nikki nodded. 'I do.'

'Well, then. . .'

'Megan, Luke won't let me near him. He won't let anyone near him.' Nikki closed her eyes, with remembered pain. 'For now. . .for now Luke wants to be alone, and I think. . .I think we have to respect that.'

'Do you think it's because he's sterile?'

Nikki looked up sharply. 'You know about that?'

Megan nodded. 'My sister was so worried, she made a special trip to Sydney to see Dr Olsing six months ago. He's the one who looked after Luke when he was ill. Dr Olsing thought that might have something to do with why. . .why he's avoiding the family.'

'Luke would have been fairly upset when he found out,' Nikki said carefully and Megan nodded again.

'Dr Olsing said there was some reason Luke couldn't bank sperm. . .and almost as soon as the last chemotherapy session was over he asked to be tested and his count was really low. Dr Olsing said if Luke hadn't been a doctor he would have pushed him to counselling but. . .well, if you know Luke you'd know he wouldn't take to counselling very well. He'd reckon he could cope. Luke hasn't been back to Dr Olsing since then. We assume he's getting his regular check-ups—but he could get them done anywhere, couldn't he?'

'I'm sure he is,' Nikki said gently. 'Luke's sensible, Megan. He'll be being careful.'

Careful and remote as the South Pole, she thought bleakly.

Megan left soon after, and Nikki faced a long and sleepless night.

In the morning she sat the first of her exams. They seemed easy, or maybe that was just because Nikki's mind was elsewhere. She answered perfunctorily and if sometimes one of her examiners seemed annoyed, well, Nikki couldn't help it.

She was nervous, though. She must be. Nikki had sat down in the hospital cafeteria for breakfast on the Monday morning only to be nauseated by the sight of so much food. She'd been ill before she'd gone into the exam. Her stomach had settled as she worked, but on Tuesday morning it happened again.

Nerves? It was almost as if. . .

The thought struck Nikki out of the blue halfway through an oral examination on bone-structure on the Tuesday afternoon. Strange sensations suddenly slid into frightening place.

Somehow Nikki managed to answer the professor's questions. There was one other written exam, which she completed in not much more than half the time stipulated. She walked out of the examination-room and didn't stop until she reached the hospital pharmacy.

An hour later Charlotte knocked on Nikki's door. Hearing no response, she turned the knob to find it unlocked. Nikki was sitting on the bed staring out of the window.

'Hey, what's this?' Charlotte chided her. 'I thought you'd be out painting the town red.' She plonked herself down on the bed beside her friend. 'Or did the exam go badly?'

'It went OK,' Nikki said listlessly.

'Well, what——?' Charlotte broke off. Her eyes caught sight of what lay on Nikki's bedside table. A small bottle, a plastic box and an eye-dropper. Charlotte leaned forward and picked up the box. The

paper in the window on the front of the box showed
a firm, definite cross.

Charlotte glanced across to where Nikki was still
staring intently out of the window, and then looked
back at the box.

'A cross,' she said conversationally. 'Who's the lucky
girl, then?'

'Charlotte, don't.' Nikki put her hands up to her
face and her shoulders heaved. With a gasp Charlotte
leaned over to grasp her friend.

'Hey, honey, don't. This isn't the end of the world.
How far. . .?'

'I'm only just,' Nikki wailed. 'I'm only a week over-
due. I just couldn't. . .'

'Luke?'

Nikki closed her eyes. 'Of course Luke,' she whispered. 'Who else?'

'Who else indeed?' Charlotte whistled silently over
Nikki's tumbled curls. 'Holy heck, Nikki, love, I
thought you had more sense.'

'I did. I do. He's supposed to be sterile. . .'

And then the whole story came tumbling out while
Charlotte's frown deepened and her hold on her
friend's shoulders tightened.

'Well,' she said at last. 'What now, Nikki Russell?'

'I don't know,' she said bleakly. 'I can't think. . .
I . . . He was so sure that he was sterile. . .'

'When was he tested?'

'I don't know,' Nikki wailed. And then she
remembered what Megan had said. 'Just. . .just after
the last lot of chemotherapy. He was very anxious.'

'Too anxious,' Charlotte said grimly. 'If he tested
too soon. . .'

'Surely he would have re-tested if he'd been nega-
tive,' Nikki whispered. 'When it was so important to
him. . .'

'Maybe that's why he didn't re-test.' Charlotte
shrugged. 'To submit yourself to a sperm count when

you think you're sterile must be pretty darned demoralising. If he got a really low count he would have assumed it would stay low. The chances of it rising are pretty darned small.'

'Small but possible,' Nikki said bleakly. 'And guess who wins the prize?'

Charlotte shook her head. 'You always were the lucky one. Nikki. . .Nikki, you realise it's early enough to do something about the pregnancy?'

'No.'

'Just like that?'

'Just like that,' Nikki told her. 'I could have done the same when I was pregnant with Amy. I was broke and frightened and much younger. And if I had, I would have missed out on my lovely daughter, and besides. . .'

'Besides?' Charlotte prompted.

'This is Luke's child.'

'I see.' Charlotte looked hard at her friend and her heart sank. Luke Marriott had claimed another victim, then. 'So tell Luke,' she said heavily. 'I've never heard that Luke Marriott didn't take his responsibilities seriously. Maybe. . .maybe he'll want to marry you.'

'For a happy-ever-after ending?' Nikki gave a short, harsh laugh. 'Is that what you think?'

'If he thinks he's sterile he'll be delighted about the baby.'

'Yes.' Nikki nodded. 'He's taken his sterility hard. And family is important to him. You're right, Charlie. If I told him, then Luke would marry me.'

'And you don't want that?'

Nikki shook her head. 'Not. . .not on those terms.'

'But he made love to you. He must feel. . .'

'He made love to me out of some crazy, stupid scheme to shake me out of my isolation and misery. For the same reason as you pinched all my clothes. Well, it worked only too well. I'm not isolated any more. I'm going to be the mother of two.'

'Oh, Nikki, will you cope?'

'Sure I'll cope,' Nikki whispered. 'The town will talk behind my back—but they always have. Beattie will stand by me. And I have my career. Isn't it lucky I've just done this damned exam?' Her voice broke on a sob and she buried her face in her hands.

'Nikki. . .' Charlotte held out a hand helplessly to her friend and then withdrew it. 'Nikki, you'll have to tell him. It's not fair. . . Apart from anything else, he has to know he's not firing blanks.'

Shaken, Nikki looked up sharply and Charlotte shrugged and grinned. 'Well, he does. . .'

'If he had a low sperm count he must only have marginal fertility,' Nikki said slowly. 'He could try for twenty years and not father another child.'

'Or he could do the same tomorrow.'

Nikki nodded. 'OK,' she said slowly. 'I'll tell him.' She took a deep breath. Her face was set. 'But not yet. I'll let him get right away from Eurong and then I'll write to him, care of the medical board. They'll forward a letter. But it won't be for a while yet. I'll give myself time to have the strength to tell him to go to blazes when he demands that I marry him.'

'That's really what you want to do?'

'He'll love our baby,' Nikki said bleakly. 'But he doesn't love me. So. . .so it's what I really have to do.'

CHAPTER TEN

NIKKI arrived back at Eurong the following afternoon to find Beattie and Amy waiting for her at the airport. Amy raced across the tarmac to envelop her mother in a bear-hug.

'Mummy, guess what? We're going to have a Luke party!'

'A Luke party.' Nikki buried her face in her daughter's chubby shoulder for longer than usual, finding comfort in that small person's presence. Another Amy? Maybe. . .maybe someone who looked like Luke. . .

'A Luke party,' she said again unsteadily, bringing her face up to smile at Beattie. 'What's a Luke party?'

'Luke's going tomorrow,' Amy told her, her face momentarily clouding. 'But Beattie said tonight we're having a party to say welcome home Mummy and goodbye Dr Luke. Only. . .only I think it would be nicer if Luke thought the party was just for him. If you don't mind?' she asked anxiously.

'I don't mind.' Nikki set her daughter back on to her feet. 'And what delicacies have we planned for such an event?'

'All the food he'll like best,' Amy said proudly. 'Little red sausages. Bread and butter and hundreds and thousands. Jelly beans. Red lemonade. Sausage rolls. . .'

'Wow!' Nikki grinned. 'What man could ask for more?'

'Exactly.' Amy skipped beside her, her hand clinging to her mother's. 'Maybe—maybe if he sees what really good food we have sometimes, maybe he'll stay.'

'I don't think that's possible.'

'No.'

Beattie glanced across at Nikki's set face and then looked away. There was real pain there.

Nikki drove down to the hospital just before dinner. Luke, it seemed, was leaving in the morning and Nikki needed to know what hospital patients were in and what their medications were while he was still available to answer questions. She did a slow ward round, methodically going through each patient's chart. There were no problems. Luke had written each patient's history with meticulous care, knowing that he was soon handing over.

The young fisherman was recovering nicely and Nikki was pleased to see his impatience to be home. 'I dunno why he's keeping me so long,' the boy complained. 'I've only got a sore thumb.'

'You wouldn't have any thumb at all if it weren't for Dr Luke,' Nikki told him severely. 'And if you risk infection by going home you can still lose it.'

'Yeah, well, I've got nine more,' the boy grinned and Nikki shook her head.

'You don't know how much you'd miss your right thumb until you're without it,' she warned him. 'So just lie back and let us take care of you.'

'It is nice,' the fisherman admitted. He smiled shyly up at her. 'The nurses here are great. And the food is something else.'

'I guess it beats your dad's cooking.' Nikki hesitated. 'Has he been in to see you?'

'Yeah, once.' The boy's face closed. 'Just wanted to know how long he'd have to hire someone else for. I dunno. . .I dunno that I'll go back to living with him. I might get private board or something.'

'Does your mum know you're in hospital?'

'No.' Jim bit his lip. 'Mum. . .well, Mum left a couple of years back and I chose to stay with Dad. It was a mistake, I guess, but. . .but I didn't know where

she was going and. . .I know Dad would hang up if
she rang, or would burn any letters she wrote.'

Nikki nodded. 'If you give me her full name and
birth-date, I might be able to contact her,' she offered.
'If you like.'

'Could you?' Jim's eyes brightened and then clouded
again. He lay back on his pillows. 'She's probably glad
to be shot of us both.'

'Let me try and see,' Nikki told him. 'It can't hurt
to try.'

She left him then and spent a fruitful half-hour on
the telephone. At the end of it she was practically
certain that the Brisbane police would contact Mrs
Payne. 'Just let her know her son's in the Eurong
hospital after suffering an accident,' she told them. It
made it sound a little more serious than it really was
now, but Jim—well, Jim was only nineteen and he still
needed someone.

Everyone does, she thought bleakly. She looked up
as the door of her office opened and Luke entered.

'Welcome back.' His tone was formal and his smile
was forced. 'How did the exam go?'

'Fine.' Nikki rose to her feet and stood awkwardly.
How would it be, she wondered, if I just told him?
Luke, I'm carrying your child. For a moment—just a
moment—she felt a crazy impulse to do so, but he
was looking at her with eyes that were distant and
formal.

'You've come for hand-over?'

'I thought I should.'

'Fine, then. Let's go.'

So they walked through the hospital again, this time
with Luke going through the notes as they visited each
patient. The process was professional, efficient
and cold.

The patients must think we can't stand each other,
Nikki thought, and bit her lip. Maybe for Luke it was
true. Nikki had made him drop his guard and let the

world in. Luke had done the same for her, but for Nikki the world, in the guise of one Luke Marriott, was more than welcome.

'Is there anything else I should know about?' she asked in a tight voice as they reached the end of the patient list.

'No. I've left notes in the surgery.'

'Fine.' She nodded hopelessly. 'I'll be getting home, then. I've. . .we've a party to organise.'

'Nikki, don't go to any trouble.'

She turned then. 'You do intend to show up?' she demanded.

'I have. . .there's a house call.'

'Luke, Amy's counting on this party.'

'Nikki, Amy has you and Beattie. . .'

'And she has you.' A surge of anger rose in Nikki. That he could hurt her was enough, but to hurt Amy. . . 'My daughter cares for you, Luke Marriott. She's as big a fool as her mother in that regard. I'd stop it if I could but I have no control over my daughter's decision to give her affection. She's sad to see you go and she's pressed us all into giving you a party that you don't deserve.'

'Nikki. . .'

'You don't care who you hurt, do you, *Mr* Marriott?' she demanded. 'You'd hurt Amy. . .you'd hurt me. You're hurting all your family—— Oh, yes, I forgot to tell you—I saw Megan while I was in Cairns. She's another whom you've hurt with your introspective nurturing of your damned pain. Just because you've been sick, Luke Marriott, you think you can trample on the feelings of others and you don't give a damn.'

'Nikki, I do. . .'

'You don't or you wouldn't do it. Amy is a lovely little girl, Luke Marriott, and she's going to cry herself to sleep tonight if you don't come to this damned party. So you can put yourself second for a change and come and eat little red sausages and party cakes and you can look as if you're enjoying it or. . .'

'Or what?' Luke's face was still.

'Or I don't know,' Nikki ended up lamely. 'Or I'll
think you're even more selfish than. . .than my ex-
husband!'

If it hadn't been for the children, the night would have
been impossible. As it was, Sandra came with her four
and the party was a riot. If Nikki was quiet and Luke's
smile was forced, then the children more than made
up for it. Sandra's brood were making up for past
deprivation with a vengeance. They ate like miniature
vultures while Sandra made futile protesting noises in
the background and Beattie looked on with an
indulgent smile.

'It does me good to see Whispering Palms full of
children,' she beamed. 'It's like it ought to be.'

She glared then at both Luke and Nikki in turn, as
if they were deliberately withholding its due from the
old house.

Afterwards the children dived *en masse* into the pool
and Luke joined them. Amy looked a question at her
mother but didn't voice it. It seemed she sensed Nikki's
reluctance to be with them. And tonight Amy was
going to enjoy her Dr Luke and her new friends to
the fullest. For tomorrow, her doubtful look at her
mother said, we'll be back to being by ourselves.

Not for long, Nikki thought grimly. Eight months?

At the thought of what lay ahead, blind panic filled
her. She had assured Charlotte that she could cope,
but could she? When Amy was a baby she had suffered
at the hands of Eurong's gossips. Now? All Eurong
would count back and know whose baby this was.

And how would Luke react when he finally found
out? He won't find out for months, Nikki told herself
desperately. It can't be until I have the strength to say
I won't be part of a family for a baby's sake. I won't. . .

And finally the interminable evening ended. Luke

left to drive Sandra and her children home and Nikki
wearily carried an exhausted Amy up to bed.

'It was nice, wasn't it?' Amy asked sleepily, snug-
gling into her mother's arms.

'Yes, it was.' Nikki pulled back Amy's bedcovers
and deposited her daughter on to the pillows. 'A
special night.'

'Dr Luke's special,' Amy said seriously. 'Mummy,
I don't think Dr Luke should go away. I think he
should stay here and be our daddy.'

And so say all of us, Nikki's heart replied. Instead,
though, she kissed her daughter goodnight and made
her way back down to the kitchen. Beattie had already
left for bed. Nikki made herself coffee and then went
to sit out by the swimming-pool. She needed time
to think.

Think of what? The next few years? The rest of her
life? She closed her eyes as loneliness engulfed her.
The responsibilities ahead were awesome and she
couldn't face them. Not alone.

There were footsteps behind her and she turned.
Luke was there, his body outlined in the light of the
doorway. He saw her and came across.

'Satisfied?' he asked her.

'That you came to my daughter's party? It was very
generous of you,' she whispered.

'I even ate little red sausages.'

As an attempt at humour it was pretty appalling but
Nikki managed a smile. She rose. 'Well done. A manly
effort.' She made to go past him but he stopped her
with his hand.

'Nikki?'

'Let me go, please,' she said steadily. 'I'm tired.'

'Nikki, I'm sorry it had to end this way. Before God,
I never meant to hurt you.'

'What did you mean to do?'

He sighed. 'I don't know, my Nikki. I saw you so
damned alone, and I thought—well, I thought it was

time you came out of your shell. So I dragged you out.'

'And now I'm exposed,' she whispered. 'Without a shell. And I'm supposed to be grateful.'

'Nikki. . .'

'I'm going to bed,' she said wearily. 'Let me go, please, Luke.'

'Not yet. . .'

'Please. . .'

'Nikki, tomorrow I'll be gone. I can't stay here. We both know that.'

Nikki shook her head. 'I don't know that. I don't see why you have to keep running.'

'I'm not running.'

'No?'

He closed his eyes. His face was haggard in the moonlight. 'Nikki, I'm just trying to come to terms with myself—with what's happened. Can't you see that?'

'With the fact that you can't have children.'

He nodded. 'Yes. It's important to me.'

'Luke. . .'

It was so close. The words were so close. Instead Nikki drew in her breath. She wouldn't buy this man's love. She wouldn't. It had to be for her. . .

'Luke, I love you,' she whispered. 'Isn't that enough? Can't that be enough?'

He stood motionless in the still, tropical night. Around them even the cicadas fell to silence, waiting. And then Luke shook his head.

'I don't think it can be,' he said roughly. 'God knows it should be. But I can't make it work. Even though I want you. . .'

'Do you want me?'

'You don't know how much.' He opened his eyes and stared across at her. She stood motionless, waiting. She was playing with every card she had. There was only tonight. There was only now.

'I'm yours if you want me, Luke,' she whispered. 'If you want me. . .'

She could do no more. She closed her eyes and waited.

And he would have had to be less than human to resist. In the moonlight, her soft white dress floating around her and her tousled curls gold-red in the moonlight, she was almost ethereal. Luke groaned and half turned away. Nikki didn't move. Please, she was whispering over and over in her heart. Please. . .

And he came to her. He had to. It was as if they were two parts of a magnetic force that only had attraction for each other. He came and gathered her into his arms as though he were drowning. His lips took hers and Nikki gave herself to him with joy.

She could never recall how it happened, but somehow. . .somehow they were inside, in her big, cool bedroom, and he was kicking the wide French windows closed behind them. Nikki's dress was somehow falling on to the polished floorboards and she was being lifted to lie on the smooth sheets, to wait. . .to wait for her love.

This was her place. This was her rightful home in the universe. She was with her man—of her man— one—and her body responded with all the joy that was in her heart.

This man was her love. This man was the father of the child she carried in her body, and her whole being reacted with light and love. Her hands took him to her, greedily, hungrily. She wanted to know every part of him, forever and ever and ever.

They were mad that night. They were two hearts, wounded and somehow made whole for the blessing of one magic night. In each other's bodies they found joy and peace and love. They made love and slept and woke and made love again and Nikki tried to keep awake in Luke's arms, so that she could savour it— this night that she wanted to go on for the rest of her life.

'I love you,' she whispered over and over again as

he loved her body—as he made her feel the most loved and wanted woman on the face of the earth. She ran her fingers over his muscled frame and sought to make him hers—sought to melt her body into his. 'I love you,' she whispered, but he didn't respond.

He didn't reply.

His lovemaking told her that he wanted her—that he needed her—and that when he was gone he would be desperate for the comfort of her body.

His tongue tasted her and loved her, but didn't say the words that would tie him to her forever.

Nothing.

And, finally, Nikki slept.

She woke at dawn as Luke stirred beside her, disengaged his body from hers and rose.

Sleepily Nikki looked up, loving the strong curves of his muscled body. Her eyes sought to know every inch of him. Instinctively she knew that there was to be no more. This was the end. The end. . .

She didn't speak. She couldn't. Instead she lay in the weak dawn light and watched the man she loved prepare to leave.

Finally, clothed, he turned to face her. Wordlessly she watched, waiting. Silence stretched out between them. It went on and on, as if neither was willing to face what had now become inevitable. Finally Luke swore softly and crossed to the bed to look down at her.

Nikki lay still, her red-blonde hair tumbled on the pillow around her too pale face. Her eyes were enormous as she looked up at him, waiting for the hurt.

And, sure enough, it came.

'Last night shouldn't have happened,' he said quietly, his eyes pain-filled. 'These whole three weeks. . .'

'Should never have happened,' Nikki agreed. 'I know. But they have, Luke. And. . .and I've changed forever because of it.'

He touched her hair as if it hurt to do so. 'I'm glad. . .if it means you'll get out more. Meet people. Find someone. . .'

'Someone who'll love me. . .' Nikki's voice broke and she turned into her pillow. 'Luke, how can you say that? How can you say that when you know I love you?'

'God, Nikki. . .'

She turned back to him then and rose to a sitting position, the sheet falling away to reveal her lovely nakedness. Her hand came out to touch his—a wordless pleading.

'Luke, why don't you want me?' She shook her head. 'I don't. . .I don't understand. You don't feel what I feel?'

'Hell!' Luke pulled his hand from hers and turned away to stand and stare out of the window. 'I want you, Nikki. God knows. . .'

'But not enough to ask me to stay with you.'

'For a while, yes,' he said bleakly. 'I want you. At this moment I want you more than anything I have ever wanted in my life. But I want more than that, Nikki. I want things I can't have. I want a family. . .'

'And I'm not enough.'

'No.' He stared sightlessly out of the window. 'For a few crazy moments here I thought it might be. I thought that with you and Amy I could be at peace. But I don't think I can ever be at peace, Nikki.'

'So the fact that you can't father a child is more important than your love for us?'

Nikki's heart shrank from what he was saying. She could have this man, she knew, just by opening her mouth and promising him his child. And it would be no better than what she had had with Scott. Scott hadn't wanted her unless she had money. Now Luke had no use for her unless she had his child.

'Nikki, it seems unfair. . .'

'It is unfair.' Nikki took a deep breath and rose,

pulling her sheet after her. She wound it around her
as if it were some sort of defence against him, but her
defence had come too late.

'You made love to me as if you loved me,' she
whispered. 'You made me feel. . .you made me feel
as if I was part of you. And I gave myself to you. Not
just my body, Luke Marriott, but myself. My love. My
heart. And now. . .now you tell me that because of
your damned past—because of an illness that's robbed
you of the ability to bear children—my love's not
enough.'

'Nikki. . .'

Anger came then, as some sort of in-built defence
against the pain. It gave her strength to lash out one
more time. 'You've got a damned nerve.' Nikki's eyes
flashed fire. 'You want me if I can bear your children,
but not otherwise. What the hell does that make me,
Luke Marriott?'

'I know. It's unfair. . .'

'Too damned right it's unfair.'

He shook his head. Luke's hands came up as if to
touch her and then fell away uselessly to his sides.

'Nikki, my family is important. . . Look, it would
be so easy to take you. To take what you're offering.
And then, in five years. . . Well, in five years, if my
inability to have children were as important to me as
it is now, we'd be in a real mess.'

'Because it would hurt for me to have Amy, and your
brothers and sisters to have children, and you not.'

'Yes. Damn it, yes.'

'And that's more important than my love. . .'

'Yes. No!' Luke was as angry as Nikki now, his eyes
almost black with frustration and fury. 'It's easy for
you to say it's not important. . .'

'And if magically you could have children. . .what
then. . .?'

He shook his head, the flash of anger slowly fading.
'I don't know,' he said quietly. 'Nikki, if I could have

children with you. . . Oh, God, Nikki. . .'

'So you'd want me as a mother to your children?'
Nikki's voice was flat and lifeless. 'But not otherwise.'

'Nikki, that's not what I'm saying.'

'Well, it's what it sounds like from here,' Nikki spat.
'It's just as well you're going, Luke Marriott. It's just
as well you're getting out of my life. Because I think
your cancer has done more damage than you know.'

'I don't know what you mean.'

'You should,' Nikki said bleakly. 'I think. . .I think
it's destroyed your capacity to love.'

'Nikki. . .'

'Just go,' she said.

CHAPTER ELEVEN

THE weeks that followed were desolate. Without Luke the house fell silent. Amy became once again a solemn child, and even Beattie forgot to sing as she did the housework.

Beattie watched her young employer with concern, her shrewd eyes taking in the tell-tale shadows on Nikki's face. If she heard Nikki wandering the house late at night, or saw her lonely figure standing out by the swimming-pool staring at nothing for hours on end, she said nothing.

Somehow Nikki managed to work. Her results came through for her examinations—'a magnificent result', the letter said. 'Congratulations!' She felt nothing. Nikki laid the letter aside and Beattie found it underneath a pile of advertising literature the following morning. Once more Beattie's forehead wrinkled into a frown of concern but still she said nothing.

It was fortunate for Nikki's sanity that there was plenty of work. She drove herself mercilessly, shoving aside the lethargy of early pregnancy. There was no time to think of the child she was carrying. She didn't want to know.

And yet, in a way, she was intensely aware of the new life starting within her. It was a little of Luke left to her. The baby would bring Luke happiness when he heard, she knew. Once he knew he was not sterile he could find someone else—one of the women who had loved him when he was back in Cairns, or someone else—someone who'd be prepared to accept him on the terms he offered. A woman who wanted to be the mother of his children first. . .

The mother of Luke's children. . . Nikki touched her

still flat stomach self-consciously as she acknowledged herself as such. That was what she was whether she wanted it or not. The mother of Luke's child. So why not accept the joy as well?

Because she wanted more. For once in her life, Nikki wanted to be loved for herself—wanted for herself—and if Luke didn't want her on those terms, then she couldn't let him near.

She began to plan the mechanics of the next few months as she went about her work. At about five months she would write to him care of the medical board, she thought—or care of the newspaper he wrote for. She would have to write before there was a possibility of his hearing via the medical grape-vine. It would be a formal little note, passing on the news of her condition and also letting him know it could make no difference to their relationship. Even if he came storming up here in another three months, then she must be strong enough to cope with that. She must be strong enough to tell him there was no place in her life for him.

'Is there anything wrong, Doc?'

Nikki looked up swiftly from what she was doing. She was re-checking Jim Payne's healing thumb. He had been released from hospital the week before, with no complications anticipated. It was healing beautifully, thanks to Luke's expert care, and Nikki forced a smile.

'Nothing's wrong, Jim,' she reassured him. 'This is looking really good. You might have some residual stiffness, but I'll give you some exercises to do once you get rid of the plaster and it'll slowly get back to almost a hundred per cent.'

'I meant——' the young man frowned down at her '—I meant with you. You're not. . .well, you're not as cheerful as you used to be.'

'I'm not a really cheerful person,' Nikki told him, somewhat taken aback at his forthrightness.

'You were when Doc Marriott was here.'

Nikki shook her head. The town would be talking about her and Luke, she knew. How much would the talk grow as her figure filled out?

'It was good to have him here,' she said simply. 'He was a very skilled surgeon.'

'Don't I know it.' Jim looked ruefully at his thumb. 'I guess I'll be grateful to him for the rest of my life.'

'You haven't heard from your mother?' Nikki asked, trying to turn the subject.

'Yeah.'

Nikki frowned. She picked up the scraps of the bandage she had been fixing and tossed them into the rubbish bin. 'So what gives?'

The boy was silent for a moment, staring at his bandaged hand. 'I dunno,' he said at last.

'You don't know.'

Jim shook his head. He looked up. 'Did you know I'm boarding at Sandra Mears's? That's. . .that's why I was saying you were more cheerful when Doc Marriott was here. Sandra said you were. She reckoned. . .she reckoned you had something going between you.'

Nikki shook her head. 'Sandra's on the wrong track,' she said tightly. Then she looked up. 'How are you finding it at Sandra's?'

'It's great. She's a real good sort. And I like the kids.'

'Mmm.' Was this going to work? Nikki turned it over in her mind, replaying the conversation she'd had with Sandra the week before.

'We advertised and Jim replied,' she'd said happily. 'And I've always felt sorry for Jimmy. I reckon he's had almost as bad a deal as me.'

'Do you think you can cope with the extra work?' Nikki had frowned and Sandra had laughed.

'I like housework,' she'd grinned. 'Call me daft if you like, but now I've a decent house to look after it'll be no trouble. The kids like Jimmy and his board money will be handy—well, I'm going to start thinking we're rich.'

So Nikki had smiled and agreed, knowing Jim was reluctant to go home to a father who didn't seem to give a damn about his only son. But if Jim's mother were to come. . .

'She telephoned me in the hospital,' Jim said slowly. 'And. . .and she asked me to go to Brisbane to stay with her.'

'Oh, Jim, that's terrific.'

He shook his head. 'Maybe not.' He looked up. 'She's remarried. Her new husband's a widower with three kids. I dunno. . .'

'You don't know where you fit?'

He shook his head. 'I know Dad seems a selfish bastard,' he said directly. 'But Mum. . .well, she left and maybe if she really wanted to contact me she could have. And here. . .well, here at least I know the people and I know I've got a job.'

'On your father's boat.'

'Yeah, well, maybe I'll go back to working for him and maybe I won't,' Jim said uncertainly. 'There's other boats. But fishing's all I know.'

'It's going to be quite a change, living with Sandra.'

'It is and all,' Jim said happily. 'Those kids. . .' He shook his head. 'They're great kids, Doc Russell, and do you know, the boys have never even been taught to kick a football?'

'No!' Nikki breathed in mock-horror and Jim grinned.

'Well, I'm going to teach them,' he said resolutely. He took a deep breath. 'Sandra's taken a risk taking me in. I know this town and I know it'll talk even more about her. But we talked it over and reckoned we could ignore it and maybe make it work.'

Nikki sat back on her heels and looked thoughtfully at the young fisherman. He sounded as if he was taking

on more of a responsibility than a decision to rent a
room for a few weeks. And when the door opened for
Jim to leave the surgery and Nikki saw Sandra and
the two youngest children in the waiting-room she saw
what was happening.

A family was forming out of mutual need. The children came forward to greet Jim as their personal
property and he took a hand of each and turned to
go. 'Thanks a lot, Doc,' he told Nikki over his shoulder. 'Thanks for everything.'

Nikki watched them walk away—Sandra at twenty-
two with the lilt of a girl back in her step and Jim at
nineteen playing the father. For heaven's sake. . .

She smiled suddenly. It might. . .it just might work.
Crazier things had happened.

And then her receptionist handed her the next card
and Nikki turned her attention to Mrs Alphington's
neuralgia. She didn't have time for reflection—and
that was the way she wanted it.

The days dragged on. Nikki found herself staring
stupidly at the calendar, as though it had some meaning. Three weeks since she had seen Luke. . . Four. . .

'When will he come back?' Amy asked for the hundredth time and Nikki strove for patience.

'Luke isn't coming back,' she said gently.

'He will,' Amy said stubbornly. 'Even if it's just for
a visit. Maybe he'll come for Christmas?'

'Don't count on it.' Nikki winced at the thought
of Christmas. She hated it. Christmas—the time of
families. Beattie left them every Christmas, flying
down to Brisbane for her once-a-year visit to her
daughter, and there would only be Amy and Nikki.
Some Christmas!

Maybe she should employ another locum—get right
away for a few weeks. If she could get somewhere
cooler, maybe this awful cloud of oppression would lift.

Summer had arrived with a vengeance—the real

tropical rainy season. It rained unceasingly, the rain turning to steam in the blistering heat. Nikki never enjoyed the rainy season and now—it was as if the sky were crying in sympathy with her.

'It's real cyclone weather,' Beattie said darkly as the first week of December neared its end. 'We're in for one, you wait and see.'

'Don't say so,' Nikki groaned. The last cyclone near Eurong had passed five years before, cutting a swath of damage. There were still scars in the rainforest from its passing.

Beattie sniffed. 'Well, there's no warnings yet. But it'll come soon.'

She was wrong. For the next few days Nikki worked with her eye on the weather and her ear constantly tuned to the local radio. Cyclone Hilda threatened them for a little, but swerved right away from the coast and blew harmlessly out to sea. There were no other warnings.

Finally Nikki ceased worrying and her thoughts went back to Luke. Where was he? How would he spend Christmas? As she and Amy put up their little Christmas tree she thought of Luke's family gathering in Melbourne. Would he visit them this year?

What would his reaction be if he knew that a child of his was on its way? That next year he would be a father. . .

A father *in absentia*, she reminded herself, and then winced. What if he demanded access? How would she cope seeing him every time he wanted to visit their child?

It didn't bear thinking of. She made herself concentrate on the silver baubles she was tying to the tree.

'It's lovely, Mummy,' Amy said in satisfaction, and then paused as Beattie hurried into the room. The housekeeper had been packing her suitcase ready for her afternoon flight south.

Something was wrong. The elderly housekeeper's

face was pale and she was obviously distressed.

'I knew it,' she said tremulously. 'It's a cyclone.'

'Oh, no.' Nikki rose, her eyes creasing in sympathy. Beattie had been filled with excitement at the thought of seeing her newest grandchild for the first time. If a cyclone was threatening between here and Brisbane then flights would be cancelled. 'How close?' Nikki asked. It wouldn't have to be too close for the plane to be cancelled.

'We're dead centre,' Beattie said grimly. 'I just heard it on the radio.'

Dead centre.

Nikki stared at Beattie in dawning horror. Dead centre of a cyclone. . . The damage cyclones did was enormous, but Eurong had never been directly in one's path. The destruction caused by being close to the cyclone path was bad enough.

'But. . .but there's been no warning of one imminent. There's only been Cyclone Hilda, and it's right out to sea, hundreds of miles north.'

'That's the one.' Beattie was practically wringing her hands. 'It's swung inland for some reason and there's a red alert. They say. . .they say it'll hit here in three hours.'

Three hours! Instinctively Nikki looked out of the window. The palms were swaying in a rising wind, but there was nothing to suggest an impending disaster.

This was no time for panic. Amy was watching with enormous eyes, and if Nikki showed she was frightened it would communicate fast to the child.

'OK,' Nikki said evenly, striving for calm. 'Let's get the storm covers up.'

'Does this mean you're not going away for Christmas, Beattie?' Amy asked, and Beattie and Nikki looked at each other. If that was all it meant they would be lucky.

'I guess it does. I. . .I think I'll take some things down to the storm cellar,' Beattie said nervously, and

Nikki nodded. They hadn't used the storm cellar for anything but storage for years. Nikki's father had installed it as a safety precaution and Eurong had decreed him mad. Totally unnecessary, they'd said, but now. . . Now, it made Nikki feel that there was at least one safe place where she could leave her daughter.

'We need to open the windows on the lee side a little,' Nikki said quietly, trying to remember the precautions she'd been taught. 'If the pressure builds up. . .'

'I know.' Beattie nodded, putting her personal disappointment aside. 'I'll do that now.'

'I'm going to have to go down to the hospital.'

'I know that too,' Beattie said grimly. She took a deep breath and looked down at Amy. 'Come on, then, young lady. You and I have got work to do.'

'Can we telephone Karen and her mum and ask them to share our cellar?' Amy bubbled. The cyclone sounded like a wonderful adventure from a four-year-old's angle.

Nikki nodded slowly. 'It's not a bad idea. Sandra's house is fibro-cement with no protection. Our cellar's big enough. . .'

'I'll telephone,' Beattie told her. She nodded decisively at Nikki, and Nikki silently blessed her good fortune at having such a competent housekeeper.

'OK.' She stooped to give Amy a quick hug. 'You promise you'll both be in the cellar an hour before the storm's due to hit—whatever happens?'

'We promise,' Beattie told her. 'And you, Nikki Russell. . .' She sighed. 'Well, take care of yourself. Don't go taking any damned fool risks.'

'Who, me?' Nikki smiled, with a bravado she was far from feeling. 'I'm not one for damned fool risks. I was born a coward.'

*   *   *

The hospital was at peak, bustling efficiency when Nikki arrived. There were three internal rooms that had no windows—the hospital had been built with storms in mind—and when Nikki arrived the nurses were moving their patients into safety.

'One room will have to be left free as Theatre,' Nikki said grimly.

'We've had enough warning for people to be prepared,' Andrea, the charge sister, said. 'Surely there won't be. . .'

'People do darned stupid things.' Nikki grimaced. 'Especially when they're frightened. And if we really are in the eye of the storm then many of these houses won't make it.'

'But most are built under regulations for cyclones.'

'Yeah.' Nikki piled boxes of dressing to carry to the makeshift theatre. 'But there's still no guarantee they'll survive the eye of a cyclone. Remember Darwin. . .'

They both did. The city had been struck on Christmas Eve several years previously and hardly a house had been left standing. The force had been as great as a major earthquake.

'It can't be as bad as that,' the nurse said nervously. 'Can it?'

'Heaven knows. I don't. Is the fishing fleet in?'

'There weren't any boats too far out to get back into harbour,' the nurse told her. 'They're all back.'

'Well, that's something.'

Nikki worked steadily, setting up her makeshift theatre as best she could. With luck the work she was doing could be totally unnecessary. To operate on seriously injured casualties. . .

She might not have a choice. Even after the cyclone passed it would be hours before the wind died enough to evacuate casualties. Nikki thought fleetingly, longingly, of Luke. She felt desperately alone, knowing the next few hours would bring more casualties than she could cope with.

'Everyone's being warned?' she asked anxiously. Her mind raced over her scores of elderly patients who lived alone. Many wouldn't have heard the radio warning.

'The State Emergency Service are doing a door-knock now,' the charge nurse told her. Andrea was linked to the emergency services by two-way radio. 'Anyone they're worried about they'll bring in here or to the school.' Like the hospital, the school also had reinforced rooms.

Fine. Everything that could be done was being done. So now there was only time to sit and wait. And hope. . .

'I don't suppose Dr Maybury could come?' Nikki said uncertainly. If she didn't have an anaesthetist there was little she could do if there were serious casualties. The elderly doctor was Nikki's nearest colleague and he was within driving distance if he came at once.

'I doubt it,' the charge sister told her. 'Penrith is thirty miles south, but by the sound of the radio warnings they're expecting damage there as well. He'll have to stay.'

Nikki nodded. She knew it already. She was on her own.

The wind rose with relentless fury.

How would Amy and Beattie be coping? Nikki tried to block out thoughts of home as the storm gathered strength. Her attention was needed here. Half an hour before the eye of the storm was due, every one of the occupants of the hospital deserted the outside rooms and the inner doors of the little hospital were wedged closed.

The telephone lines were already down. There was no way Nikki could contact home, even if she wanted to. Eurong was isolated until the storm was past, and every home was also completely isolated.

As they closed the big inner doors and Nikki saw the outside world for the last time, she wondered how on earth the storm could get fiercer. The huge coconut palms around the hospital were bending almost double in the shrieking wind and, beyond the headland, the sea was a seething white fury.

But grow worse it did. Locked behind their doors, the hospital occupants couldn't see but they could hear. The wind screamed around the little building and every now and then a crack rang out like gunfire—the sound of a palm giving up its fight for life.

There was little time to listen. Within the room Nikki's patients were terrified—not so much for the immediate danger but at the thought of what lay ahead when those doors were opened again. Nikki moved from bed to bed, comforting as best she could and listening to nameless fears. She sedated one elderly lady as her fears brought on angina. A full-scale heart attack was the last thing Nikki wanted now. She would have enough to deal with when the doors opened.

The wait was interminable. The sound of the screaming wind went on and on, and when it finally eased Nikki knew that the doors had to stay closed.

Now they were in the eye of the cyclone—and there was a rim to the eye. They had passed through one side of the rim, and the other was yet to come.

If only she knew what was going on at home. . . The thought of the cellar was infinitely comforting. And Beattie knew about the eye of the storm. She knew not to come out yet. The little radio owned by one of the patients and listened to by all was blazing out warnings of the danger to come. 'Stay where you are,' it warned over and over again. 'Don't think the danger is over. Stay behind closed doors. Use rooms with the least windows. Think of the pantry—or the broom closet. The bathroom is often the safest room. Stay where you are. . .'

As long as people were listening. Nikki sent endless

silent prayers up to whoever would listen. Please let
people stay put. Please let no one be hit by falling
trees or flying pieces of corrugated iron. . . It was a
useless prayer but she sent it anyway.

'I won't have a house any more,' an elderly man
said flatly as she paused by his bed. 'My place is old
and run-down, and it won't stand up to this racket.'
His gnarled old face creased into tears. 'You'll have
to put me in a home after this. My house'll be
matchsticks.'

There was little comfort Nikki could give. Outside
the storm struck again as the eye passed and each fresh
blast made her wince. To stay here while Eurong was
blown to bits. . .it was the hardest thing she had done
in her life.

And then, finally, the worst of the storm was past.
The screaming wind settled to howls, and then to a
dull whine. The nurses looked at each other fearfully
and then at Nikki. Nikki nodded in silent acquiescence.
It was time to open the doors.

Maybe it would have been better to stay inside. The
nurses and the ambulatory patients walked outside to
a deathless hush. It was a frightening new world.

The hospital had survived. The building was intact,
but every window had been blasted out. The rooms
were full of debris and rain water. Torn curtains lay
shredded on the floor in sodden heaps. The wind still
whistled in through the broken windows, bringing rain
in with it. Steam rose from everything.

Soundlessly they moved outside. The veranda posts
had crumpled under the strain and the roof sagged
under the weight of a huge coconut palm. Luckily the
two posts over the door had held so it was safe to
move outside.

If one wanted to. Nikki took one look and decided
she might not want to see the rest of the devastation.
The hospital gardens were in ruins. Nikki's car lay
where she had parked in the hospital car park, turned

up on to its side. It was covered with a mass of torn
and twisted debris.

'Dear God.' Andrea was beside Nikki and her hand
came up to grasp Nikki's arm. 'Dear God. . .'

There was nothing else to say.

Around them the rest of the staff were slowly coming
to terms with what they were seeing. They had little
time for reflection. As the patients saw and guessed
at the damage elsewhere it was as much as the small
nursing staff could do to control the rising hysteria.

Nikki conquered it by ordering everyone to work,
patients included.

'I want everyone fit enough to move to start getting
the water out of the wards,' she demanded. 'I want
plastic over the windows. I want the beds made
up again dry and ready for whatever comes. Mrs
Fletcher. . .' Nikki eyed a patient who'd been in hospital with a broken hip. Mavis Fletcher was in tears
already and her tears were turning to noisy sobs.
'Mavis, can you hear me?'

Mavis looked up tearfully. 'Oh, me dear,' she
gasped. 'What are we going to do? What are we
going to do?'

'I don't know about you but I intend to start working,' Nikki said grimly. 'If I'm not mistaken there'll
be people out there who are a lot worse off than we
are. If I put you in a wheelchair, can you supervise
sandwich-making? Mr Roberts might be able to help.
What do you say?'

Mavis gave a tearful gulp. She looked around at the
mess and then back to Nikki. To be needed. . .

'If you think I can, dear,' she whispered.

Nikki grinned. 'I'm sure you can,' she said solidly.
'I'm sure we all can.'

It was the last time Nikki had to ask anyone to help.
The whole hospital was galvanised into action, even
the patients doing what they could to clear the mess
and prepare for the onslaught.

And onslaught there was. Five minutes after they emerged from the inner rooms their first casualty arrived—a man carrying his three-year-old daughter. She'd been hit by a block of plaster falling from the roof. The child was concussed and needed stitches to a nasty gash on her head, and by the time Nikki had attended her there were three more patients waiting.

Amazingly there seemed little serious injury. As each casualty arrived Nikki braced herself for tragedy, but, although the stories of property damage were heartbreaking, as yet there were no reports of loss of life. There were a couple of fractures and dozens of lacerations caused by falling debris. Nikki held her breath as she worked. If this was all. . .

'The new regulations seem to have worked,' Andrea told her in a break between patients. 'And the warnings which everyone's had since Darwin. People haven't taken risks, and they haven't been seriously hurt.'

Nikki nodded. 'Andrea, could you find out about Whispering Palms?' she said tightly. The girl working beside her flashed her a look of understanding.

'Oh, Doctor, I'm sorry. I'll contact SES. They'll go around now.'

'There's no need to make a special trip,' Nikki managed. 'But. . .but I'll work better if I know it's still standing.'

'Of course.' Andrea turned to go but before she did they heard footsteps racing along the debris-strewn hall and the door to their inner sanctum burst open.

It was Sandra.

Sandra was soaking wet, her dress was torn and a gash dripped blood slowly down across one eye. She was wild-eyed and gasping for breath.

'Nikki,' she burst out. 'Doctor. . .Nikki, can you come. . .?'

Nikki turned from the wound she was dressing. The colour drained from her face. Sandra had been in the cellar at Whispering Palms.

'Amy,' she whispered. She clutched the edge of the examination table. 'Sandra, where's Amy?'

Sandra caught herself with a visible effort. She took a ragged breath and then another. Silently Andrea moved forward and took the girl's arm. She looked as though she was about to collapse.

'It's not Amy,' she managed. 'I'm. . .I'm sorry. I didn't think. . .'

'You were in the cellar at Whispering Palms?'

Sandra nodded. Andrea pushed the girl into a chair and she sat gratefully, her knees buckling under her. 'Th-thanks.'

'OK.' Now that Nikki's worst fear had been relieved she could be calm again. She knelt in front of Sandra and took her hands. 'Tell me what's happened,' she said gently.

'It's Jim. . .'

'Jim Payne.'

Sandra nodded. 'He was with us at the beginning. Helping with the kids. Then, when Beattie rang, he said it was sensible that we all go to Whispering Palms. So he took us.'

'But he didn't stay?'

Sandra shook her head. 'He wouldn't. He. . .he made sure we were all safe and made us promise not to leave the cellar. And then he said he had to go to his father. . .'

His father. Nikki thought of Bert Payne's tiny run-down house down by the beach. Whatever regulations the council had introduced, she could be a hundred per cent sure that Bert wouldn't have introduced them. He'd tell any official to mind his own damned business.

'So Jim's down at his father's.'

'No. Yes.' Sandra looked up, her face a tear-stained plea for help. 'As soon as we got out of the cellar I went to try to find him. Whispering Palms is OK and Beattie said she'd be fine with the kids. And. . .and Jim's been so good to us. I had to leave the car a quarter of a mile from the house and walk in. There's trees down all over. And then. . .then I came to the house.' She looked up. 'It's down.'

'The house has collapsed?'

'Yes.'

'And Jim and his father are inside.'

'Yes.'

Nikki's grip on the girl's hands tightened. 'Are they dead, Sandra?'

The shock tactics worked. Sandra's eyes flew open and she fought for some sort of control. She shook her head. 'Not. . .not yet. I. . . Will you come?'

'Of course I'll come.' Nikki was already rising, pulling Sandra after her. 'Are they trapped inside?'

'I don't. . .' Again a ragged gasp for breath. 'Yes. There's a huge tree over the house. And Jim's inside and his father's stuck fast. And Jim says he'll bleed to death if he leaves him, but the tree's going to come all the way down any minute, and. . .'

'Let's go.' Nikki turned to Andrea. 'Let the emergency services know. I want able-bodied men there as fast as possible. Tell them I want shoring timbers and as much help as I can get.'

'Do you want me to come?' Andrea asked.

Nikki shook her head. 'You're needed here, Andrea. I'm needed here too, come to that, but if Bert Payne's bleeding. . .' She turned back to Sandra. 'Does anyone else know?'

Sandra shook her head. 'I. . . It was closer to run to the hospital than go back for the car. I didn't meet anyone. . .'

'OK. Let's go.'

They arrived at what was left of Bert Payne's fishing shack ten minutes later. The road was impassable with Nikki's little car, but just as they came to a halt three men in a State Emergency four-wheel-drive vehicle came racing up behind them. They moved Nikki's equipment over to their Jeep and kept on going.

'Good grief,' Nikki muttered, holding on to her seat for dear life. The Jeep bucketed over the debris, strewn as if it were a deliberately placed obstacle course. 'You'll kill this car.' She blinked forward, trying to see what was ahead in the pelting tropical rain.

'Better the Jeep dies than Jim Payne,' the driver said grimly and Nikki nodded. Jim. . . There was concern for the boy but not the father. Bert Payne had made few friends in this town.

Then what was left of Bert Payne's house was in view and the condition of the Jeep was forgotten.

The house was flattened as if it had been a house of cards, blown flat. Nikki stared at the wreck in horror. There were the remains of a chimney-stack in one corner and nothing else. There was nothing higher than chest height. That someone might still be in there. . .

The driving wind and rain were almost blinding her, whipping her sodden hair around her face. Nikki pushed it back in frustration. Before the Jeep came to a halt Sandra was out of the vehicle, running to what was left.

'Jim!' she screamed. 'Jim. . .'

'Sandra. . .' It was a hoarse cry from somewhere under the ruin, barely audible above the sound of the still whistling wind. 'Sandra. . .'

'I've got help,' Sandra yelled hoarsely. 'Dr Nikki. And men. . .'

Already the men were in action, following the sound of Jim's voice. Nikki dragged her bag from the car and then stood helplessly. Where on earth were they?

'They're right under the tree,' Sandra said hopelessly. 'Oh, God. . .'

The tree was enormous. It was a vast strangler fig, which had grown originally around a coconut palm. The coconut palm had long since died and the fallen fig now resembled a huge hollow log after the rotting of its host. It was almost twenty feet wide at the base—a mass of thick, twisting wood, smashed down on the tiny house.

'We're going to have to cut through,' the SES chief said grimly. 'We'll never lift the thing.'

'It's going to come down further,' Sandra told him. 'Look. . .'

They looked. Where the tree had snapped was about eight feet from the base. It had fallen but the base of its broken part had caught on the shattered stump. There was maybe a two-inch rim where the weight of the huge tree rested.

'My God. . .' the SES chief whispered. He swung around to his second-in-command. 'The shoring timbers we've got won't hold that. Get back to base. I want more men and stouter timbers. If that goes down. . .'

There was no reason to finish the sentence. They all knew.

'Jim, where are you?' Nikki was moving along the trunk of the tree, stepping over debris.

'In here. . .' Jim's voice was hoarse and tight.

'Are you hurt?'

'Yeah. . . I've. . .I think my arm's broke. . . And my head. . .I keep blacking out. . .'

'And your dad?'

'He's here. He's unconscious but he's still alive. He's bleeding, though, Doc. I'm holding his leg but. . .I can't keep the pressure up.'

'Are you trapped?'

'There's a bit of space behind me. I reckon. . .I reckon I could crawl back out. But. . .but Dad's stuck and if I leave him he'll bleed to death.'

Nikki was standing almost over the voice now. She looked around to where the debris subsided. The old doorway was just here. . .

Clambering down, she peered through. There was a gap in here. If she crawled. . .

'Jim. . .?'

'Yeah. . .'

She could see a shape stir slightly in the blackness. The beams of the doorway had slipped down but had afforded protection to a small area—a tunnel of no more than eighteen inches in diameter. Jim seemed about fifteen feet in through this tunnel.

'Your father's bleeding from the leg?' she asked. Behind her, the SES men and Sandra were staring in horror as she wedged herself into the gap, trying to see.

'The top of his thigh. He's. . . The tree's over his chest. I can't budge. . .' Jim's voice trailed off. He sounded close to unconsciousness himself.

'And you've lost blood too?' Nikki spoke loudly and insistently. She didn't want him passing out now.

'Yeah. . . It. . .it doesn't matter. . .'

'Oh, Jim.' Behind Nikki, Sandra had started to cry. She clutched Nikki's arm and pulled her backwards. 'He's got to come out. If that tree slips. . .' Then she raised her voice. 'Jim, you've got to come out. Your dad doesn't give a stuff about you. You've got to——' She broke off and turned away.

'Jim's not like his father,' Nikki told her, rising and putting her hand briefly on Sandra's shoulder. 'And if he were. . .if he were then you wouldn't be crying.' She took a deep breath and lowered her voice. 'Sandra, have you told Jim how dangerous the tree is?'

Sandra shook her head. 'I didn't see until now. Oh, Nikki. . .'

'Jim, we're shoring up the entrance to where you are.' Nikki gave a warning look to Sandra and the men as she raised her voice. 'I want you to come out.'

'I'm not leaving. I told you. . . Dad'll die.'

'He'll die if you stay,' Nikki said brutally. 'You sound as though you're drifting in and out of unconsciousness. 'Do you have the strength to maintain pressure on that leg, or is it still bleeding?'

'It's still bleeding,' Jim managed.

'But you can move?'

'Yeah. . .but. . .'

'Jim, I can't get in unless you come out,' Nikki said harshly. 'And your father needs me.'

Sandra gave a gasp. 'But Nikki. . . You can't. . .'

She was stopped by Nikki's fierce grip on her arm. 'Sandra, Jim's hurt and I don't know how badly. This is the only way he'll come out.'

It was. Nikki had known it since she saw the entrance. It was unpalatable but true. She bent down and peered into the recess. One of the SES men was directing a flashlight through the rubble. 'OK, Jim,' she ordered. 'Start moving slowly backwards. Now!'

'But Dad'll die. . .'

'The faster you get out, the faster I get in,' Nikki said ruthlessly. 'Move, Jim.'

Three minutes later Jim emerged to daylight. Nikki did a lightning check on the dazed young man, satisfied herself that she could leave him to the care of the people around him, and then stooped down. The SES man stopped her as she placed her hand on the door-beam.

'Doc, this is just Bert Payne you're risking your neck for,' he said uncertainly. 'I. . .I don't like this. . .'

Nikki nodded. 'I know it's just Bert Payne,' she whispered, looking over to where Sandra was holding Jim. 'But he's dying in there, and I'm a doctor. I haven't a choice.'

'He wouldn't do the same for you,' the man said brutally.

'No.' Nikki shook her head. 'But then he doesn't seem to have passed his cruel attitudes on to his son, thank heaven. . . And we can't afford to be like him.' She took one last look at Jim and Sandra, took a deep breath and lowered herself into the makeshift passage.

Jim had been wearing heavy denim jeans, which had protected him a little from the worst of the jagged splinters and nails, and for the first time in weeks Nikki regretted that she wasn't wearing the same. Charlotte's pretty clothes had become part of her—a legacy of her time with Luke. Now the dress she was wearing ripped three feet into the tunnel and she felt a nail jab into her bare leg. She swore and kept going.

I'll ring Charlotte and give her a hard time when I get out of here, Nikki thought grimly as she felt her way forward through the mass of broken timber. The thought of Charlotte—of Cairns—of somewhere other than this hell-hole—was somehow steadying. She had to think of something other than the tree poised above.

Where on earth was Bert? Jim had backed out this way. Bert Payne must be somewhere here. . .

She shoved forward, her hands groping in the dim light, and her hand met something soft. Here he was. . .

Nikki could see nothing. What she was feeling seemed to be a leg. She'd attached a rope to her waist before coming in, and now she turned to tug it after her. Her bag came sliding roughly through the debris, and attached to its handle was a flashlight. Nikki looked back along the tunnel and saw daylight being blocked by anxious faces. She flashed her light at them and then turned back to her patient.

And her heart sank. Bert Payne lay half crushed by the huge tree. It held his body in a vice, and Nikki couldn't see his left arm or leg. His face was near her, his skin devoid of any colour, and his breathing was shallow and uneven. Nikki's hand slid down the exposed leg, and met the warm ooze of blood.

Instinctively Nikki felt for a pressure point, but she knew already that her action was useless. There must be massive internal injuries. With her free hand she felt for a pulse, and as she did Bert's eyes flew open.

'Jim. . .' he whispered.

'We've taken Jim out,' Nikki said gently. 'He has a broken arm, but he's safe.'

'But. . .' The man's eyes concentrated in a sheer

effort of remembrance as Nikki groped in her bag for morphine. 'But he was here. . .'

'Yes.'

'He came back to see I was all right. . .'

'Yes, he did.' Nikki twisted her body to a position where she could fill the syringe. She turned and drove it home, wondering as she did so whether there was time for it to take effect.

'I was. . .I was a bastard to him,' the big man muttered. He reached forward with his one free arm and gripped Nikki's hand. 'You're sure. . .you're sure he's all right?'

'He's safe.' Nikki was no longer worrying about the oozing blood. It was too late for that now. She gripped Bert's free hand in hers and held it.

'Tell him. . .tell him I'm sorry.'

'I'll do that,' Nikki told him evenly. 'I promise.'

'And tell him. . .' The elderly fisherman closed his eyes as if he had reached a point where he could go no further. His words were an almost superhuman effort. 'Tell him he's been a good kid and I'm. . .I'm proud of him. Tell him. . .'

'I'll tell him.'

It was the last thing Bert Payne ever said. Five minutes later he died.

There was nothing more for Nikki to do. She let Bert's hand rest on the pile of rubble, and pushed her bag back out of the way. There was no point in her staying. Not now. . .

But as she moved so did the tree. Nikki looked up in fear as the massive trunk started slowly to settle. She flung herself backwards, but it was too late.

The mass of rubble in the tunnel behind her came down in a dust-laden roar. The dust filled her head, blinding her. She put her hands instinctively to her head and waited.

And it came. The huge mass of debris above her head shifted downwards. Nikki felt a blow to her shoulder and then a massive, crushing weight on her head. She tried to cry out, but no sound came. The weight. . .

'Nikki!' The sound came from outside the shifting rubble. 'Nikki. . .'

'Luke. . .' Nikki whispered a response uselessly into the shifting, tearing dark. It was Luke. He had come back to her. . . 'Luke. . .'

Then she knew no more.

CHAPTER TWELVE

THERE was something gripping her head. It was an iron vice, clamping behind each ear and slowly squeezing. . .

Nikki opened one eye and then shut it again fast. Whatever was holding her gripped a thousandfold tighter with light. She lay absolutely still, not daring to move. Whatever vice her torturers were using might stay in abeyance if she only kept still.

'There's my girl. Come on, Nikki, love. You can do it. Come on, my love.'

She was dead and was dreaming. Nikki's eyes stayed firmly closed while she thought about the voice.

It was Luke's. It was Luke's voice. Her love. . .

Maybe it was. . . Maybe. . . Maybe if she opened her eyes she would see him, but then again, maybe not. Maybe she was dead and dreaming.

'Come on, Nikki, love.' There was no mistaking the voice. Nikki felt her hands being taken between two strong ones, and gripped. And somehow Luke's hold on her hands lessened the gripping pain surrounding her head.

'Come on, Nikki, love. You can do it. Come back to me, Nikki.'

'Come back to me'. . . Still Nikki didn't stir. She lay and let the voice drift around her.

It was Luke. He was here, with her, and his voice held love.

If she opened her eyes then she might find it was all a dream. That it was all some cruel joke. Her head hurt so. . .

A tear crept down her cheek and she tasted it as it

181

reached her lips. She was dead and dreaming that Luke
was here. . .that Luke had come back to her. . .

And then the hold on her hands tightened and a
mouth covered hers, kissing away the salt tear. 'Come
on, Nikki, love. Come back to me. I love you so
much. . .'

And she opened her eyes.

It was no dream. He was here—her Luke. He was
holding her as if she were the most precious thing in
the world, and his kiss held the tenderness she had
only dreamed of.

He must have felt her slight movement. Luke's head
lifted from her face and his troubled eyes looked down.
And he saw her eyes on his.

There was no mistaking the joy in his face. It lit him
within, blazing down on her like a blessing.

'Nikki. . .' His voice was hoarse with strain.
'Nikki. . .'

'Luke. . .' Nikki wasn't too sure where her voice
came from. She only knew that somehow the nightmare had receded. The pain in her head was still there
but so was Luke—and who could feel pain with so
much happiness inside?

Tears slid helplessly down her face. 'Luke,' she whispered again, and he closed her lips with his fingers.

'Don't try to speak, Nikki, love. You're safe. Amy
and Beattie are fine. And you're safe. That's all that
matters.'

'You came. . .'

'Too damned right I came,' Luke said grimly. He
gathered her tenderly to him, holding her tight while
leaving her carefully still on the white hospital bed-
clothes. 'And I'm never leaving you again. Not ever.
And that's a promise, my love.'

'My love'. . . Nikki closed her eyes again as the
words drifted round and round her. 'My love'. . .

It was with her still as she drifted into sleep.

* * *

When next she woke the pain in her head had all but disappeared. Nikki lay for a moment staring sightlessly up at the hospital ceiling. The pain had gone, but so had Luke.

Had she dreamed the whole thing? Had it been some crazy nightmare. . .?

She put her hand tentatively up to her head. A large bandage covered her forehead. She'd been hit on the head and had been dreaming.

The disappointment almost made her cry out, but as her hand dropped to the pillow the door opened and Andrea bustled in.

'Well, well,' the charge nurse smiled. 'So you're awake, Dr Russell. About time too.'

Nikki tried to focus. 'How. . .how long have I been asleep?'

'Oh, about two days.'

Two days!

'Well, not all of that time asleep,' Andrea told her, lifting Nikki's wrist and looking down at her watch to check her pulse. 'You were unconscious for twenty-four hours.' She grimaced down. 'You gave us the fright of our lives,' she confessed.

'I gave me the fright of my life,' Nikki agreed weakly. She put her hand back up to her bandages. 'What's. . .?'

'A fractured skull and twelve stitches,' Andrea told her. 'But it's a simple fracture and there doesn't appear to be any internal bleeding. Dr Luke says——'

'Dr Luke. . .?'

'Dr Luke says you'll live.' Andrea grinned happily down at Nikki. 'And Dr Luke seems a whole heap happier since he made that announcement, I can tell you.'

'So he really is here. I. . .I thought I dreamed it.'

'He's here,' Andrea told her. 'He's checking a plaster at the moment or he'd probably be beside you right now.' She smiled again. 'He's spent a fair amount of time next to this bed over the last two days.'

'I. . .I thought I heard him when. . .when the tree came down.'

'You did,' Andrea told her. 'I gather he was in Cairns and when the cyclone warning came through he moved heaven and hell to get back here. He came storming in here about fifteen minutes after you left for Bert Payne's. He got a helicopter to Port Douglas, but heaven knows how he got through the blocked roads to here. The call came from the SES people about two minutes after he arrived, asking for more men and longer shoring timbers and telling us why. They told us you were in the ruins with Bert, and Dr Marriott. . .well. . .' She shook her head. 'I think Dr Marriott seemed a little crazy.'

'So he was there. . .'

'He got there just as the tree came down,' Andrea told her. 'The SES men told me he worked like a madman.' She hesitated. 'Have a look at his hands next time you see him. They're torn to bits. He didn't stop until they got you out, and even then. . .well, even then I think he was a little crazy.' She shook her head. 'You looked awful. You were deeply unconscious and there was so much blood. . .'

'But Bert Payne. . .'

'Bert Payne's dead,' Andrea told her. 'But Jim's alive, thanks to you. The SES people say it was a miracle you weren't crushed to death. Anyone as big as Jim would be dead for sure.'

'Jim's. . . Jim's OK?'

'Jim's OK. It's his plaster Dr Marriott is checking now.'

'It's checked.' The strongly masculine voice came from the doorway, making the charge nurse twist around with a start. Luke was standing there, his stethoscope swinging from his fingers and his eyes on Nikki. 'He needs a new sling, though, Sister,' he said without taking his eyes from Nikki. 'If you could.'

The charge nurse looked from Nikki to Luke and back again. She smiled broadly. 'I was just taking Dr Russell's obs,' she said demurely. 'But if you think my services are wanted elsewhere. . .'

'I think your services are wanted elsewhere,' Luke confirmed.

'You won't disturb my patient, will you, Doctor?' the nurse grinned. Luke picked up the observation chart threateningly.

'Get out of here, you insolent baggage,' he smiled. 'Dr Russell, I'm sorry to inform you that you have a very insubordinate staff.'

'It's hard to command respect when Andrea and I went to kindergarten together,' Nikki whispered, and Luke crossed swiftly to the bed to take her hand. Behind him Andrea made her departure, still grinning.

'Don't you worry about that, my love,' he said gently. 'The staff'll fall in line now I'm back working here. Together we'll pull this place into shape.' He smiled down at the bed in a way that made Nikki's heart almost stop beating.

'Together'. . . And Luke was looking at her as. . . as she had always dreamed a man would look at her.

Not just a man. Her Luke.

'We. . .' she whispered.

'This medical service is damned inefficient,' Luke complained with mock-severity. He sat on the bedside chair and possessed himself of her other hand. 'Leaking roofs. Draughty corridors. Nurses wearing torn jeans and swearing their uniform blew out the window when I complain. A hospital kitchen with a living pot-plant wedged right through one wall. I like a bit more anti-septic and sparkle myself. A staff who say, "Yes, Doctor, no, Doctor, three bags full, Doctor."'

'You don't stand a chance in a million,' Nikki smiled. 'But. . .but, Luke. . .'

'Yes, my love?' His eyes were twisting her in two.

His eyes were making love to her all by themselves.

'You're not staying?'

Luke frowned. 'Nikki, Whispering Palms is one of the few undamaged houses in the district. You don't have any reason to leave.'

'I. . . N-no.'

'Well, there you go, then. You're staying. I'm staying.'

'Luke. . .' Nikki looked helplessly up at him. Her head was spinning in a dizzy haze of light. 'Luke, don't. . .don't say it. . .'

'Don't say it isn't true,' he finished for her. He nodded and his smile faded. His grip on her hands tightened. 'I shouldn't. But I can be happy here. There's enough medicine to keep me content, and I can keep my journalism going as well. But whether I stay depends.'

'Depends?'

'On whether one crazy, courageous, beautiful girl-woman will find it in her heart to forgive me for walking away on the most precious gift I've ever received. On whether my heart. . .my life. . .my lovely Nikki will marry me.'

Nikki drew in her breath. 'Luke. . .'

'I know I left you,' Luke said softly. 'But, Nikki, I almost went out of my mind. I thought. . .I thought family was so damned important. My masculinity was such an issue that I couldn't cope. And then. . .then I walked away and I realised you and Amy were my family already, whether you agreed to marry me or not. Because my heart is yours, Nikki Russell. For now and forever.'

Nikki took a long, shuddering breath. Tears of weakness and joy were sliding down her face and Luke swore as he bent to kiss them away.

'You don't have to say anything yet,' he told her gently. 'God, Nikki, I shouldn't be saying this. But. . . but I thought I'd lost you. And I thought there was nothing as bad as that. The cancer. Infertility. Nothing. To lose my lovely Nikki. . .' He shook his head and then kissed her lightly on the lips. 'You need to sleep. We can talk about this later.'

'Yes. . .' It was a sleepy murmur. Nikki's hand didn't relinquish her grip, and her hand was not relinquished in turn. She was where she wanted to be for the rest of her life.

'Nikki, love. . .'

'Mmm?'

'Nikki, before you sleep, can you do a wriggle for me? Test your fingers and toes.'

Nikki thought about this for a moment. It was sensible, and it didn't interfere with her euphoric happiness. She tried.

'Ouch,' she said softly.

'Where?'

'I've got full movement,' she told him sleepily. 'But my lower back feels as though it's been kicked by a horse.'

'You've got a thumping bruise there,' Luke told her. 'It looks like just bruising, but maybe I'd better take an X-ray to make sure.'

Nikki's eyes flew wide suddenly. 'Luke. . .Luke, I haven't been bleeding, have I?'

He frowned. 'No. Apart from your head.'

She closed her eyes in thankfulness. 'Thank God,' she whispered.

'Thank. . .' Luke let her hands fall and he bent forward. 'Nikki, what the hell. . .?'

She smiled faintly and her eyes opened again. This was right. There would never be a better time.

'I was just thinking maybe you shouldn't do that X-ray,' she whispered.

'Why not?' Luke's eyes were dark with anxiety.

'Because pelvic X-rays on unborn babies are contra-indicated.'

'Unborn babies.' Luke sat back hard in his chair.

'You mean. . . My God, Nikki, you're not pregnant?'

'Only a little bit.' She smiled shyly.

'Only. . .' He seized her hands again and his grip wasn't gentle. 'How far?'

'You tell me,' Nikki smiled. 'Or don't you remember?'

There was a long, long silence. Nikki watched as Luke's face twisted. His eyes closed, as though in pain.

But when they opened there was no pain. There was joy. There was love. And there was peace.

'My Nikki. . .'

He gathered her to him and held her close. Around them the insistent rain battered the roof and the wind whipped around the building searching for entry in the makeshift repairs.

Neither noticed. No storm could touch them where they were.

They had come home.

10th anniversary

Temptation is Ten!

Join the festivities as Mills & Boon celebrates Temptation's tenth anniversary in February 1995.

There's a whole host of in-book competitions and special offers with some great prizes to be won—watch this space for more details!

In March, we have a sizzling new mini-series Lost Loves about love lost...love found. And, of course, the Temptation range continues to offer you fun, sensual exciting stories all year round.

After ten tempting years, nobody can resist

Temptation 10th anniversary

 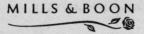

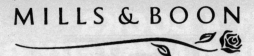

MILLS & BOON

LOVE CALL

The books for enjoyment this month are:

STORM HAVEN Marion Lennox
IN AT THE DEEP END Laura MacDonald
NO LONGER A STRANGER Margaret O'Neill
KNIGHT'S MOVE Flora Sinclair

♥   ♥   ♥   ♥   ♥

Treats in store!

Watch next month for the following
absorbing stories:

ANYONE CAN DREAM Caroline Anderson
SECRETS TO KEEP Josie Metcalfe
UNRULY HEART Meredith Webber
CASUALTY OF PASSION Sharon Wirdnam

Available from W.H. Smith, John Menzies, Volume One,
Forbuoys, Martins, Tesco, Asda, Safeway and other
paperback stockists.

Also available from Mills & Boon Reader Service,
Freepost, P.O. Box 236, Croydon, Surrey CR9 9EL.

Readers in South Africa - write to:
IBS, Private Bag X3010, Randburg 2125.

GET 4 BOOKS
AND A MYSTERY GIFT

Return the coupon below and we'll send you 4 Love on Call novels absolutely FREE! We'll even pay the postage and packing for you.

We're making you this offer to introduce you to the benefits of Reader Service: FREE home delivery of brand-new Love on Call novels at least a month before they are available in the shops, FREE gifts and a monthly Newsletter packed with information.

Accepting these FREE books places you under no obligation to buy you may cancel at any time, even after receiving just your free shipment. Simply complete the coupon below and send it to:

HARLEQUIN MILLS & BOON, **FREEPOST**, PO BOX 70, CROYDON CR9 9EL.

- -

Yes, please send me 4 Love on Call novels and a mystery gift as explained above. Please also reserve a subscription for me. If I decide to subscribe I shall receive 4 superb new titles every month for just £7.20* postage and packing free. I understand that I am under no obligation whatsoever. I may cancel or suspend my subscription at any time simply by writing to you but the free books and gift will be mine to keep in any case.
I am over 18 years of age.

1EP5

Ms/Mrs/Miss/Mr _____

Address _____

_____

_____ Postcode _____